Who will be the next to disappear?

I was ready to quit. No matter what I had promised in the beginning, now I just wanted out. I had my mouth open to tell them that this was the end, that we were fooling around with real danger, when Sara gave a little cry that froze me. I couldn't move.

"No!" Sara said. "There's something wrong here!"

Allie moved closer to me, and Roberta turned to stare at Sara.

"What's the matter?" Roberta whispered.

Sara began to shake. "There's something fearful in this room! There's something terrible! Don't you feel it?"

Dana let out a strangled gasp. "Don't do that, Sara! You're scaring me!"

Sara's voice grew louder, and she got up on her knees, her hands clawing the air. I was halfway up myself, trying to break loose from Allie's frantic grip, when Sara suddenly screamed a bloodcurdling yell and fell forward on the candle, snuffing out the only light in the house.

The Séance

JOAN LOWERY NIXON

Published by
Dell Publishing
a division of
Bantam Doubleday Dell Publishing Group, Inc.
666 Fifth Avenue
New York, New York 10103

The trademark Laurel-Leaf Library® is registered in the U.S. Patent
and Trademark Office.

The trademark Dell® is registered in the U.S. Patent and Trademark
Office.

ISBN: 0-440-97937-4

RL: 5.5

Reprinted by arrangement with Harcourt Brace Jovanovich,
Publishers

Printed in the United States of America

One Previous Edition

July 1992

20   19   18   17   16   15   14   13   12

RAD

The Séance

1

I melted back from the window to keep my night-gown from reflecting the pale light of the swelling moon, flattening myself against the ridged window frame. I held my shoulder where the sharp edge of wood had rubbed it and watched Sara Martin sneak home.

A car had rolled up to park in front of our gate, its lights cut but the engine still running, and the sound had awakened me. Sometimes the guys Sara went out to meet dropped her off at the corner. This one had taken her all the way home.

As the front door on the passenger side swung open, I turned away. I didn't want to see who the driver was. Above all, I didn't want to see Sara kiss him good-night.

Slowly I climbed back into bed. I heard the car

drive away, and soon there was a tiny click-squeak as the front door opened and shut. Sara climbed the stairs and went to her room with no more noise than a cat kneading a cushion before curling into it. She thought no one heard her comings and goings, but I'm a light sleeper, unlike Aunt Mel, and Sara's after-dark movements had become a new pattern in my nights, mixed with waking and dreaming and a strange, desperate, hurting feeling of being totally alone.

I was sorry Sara had come into the life I shared in this big house with Aunt Mel.

Aunt Melvamay, my mother's aunt, has been parenting me since I was four, when my mother died. My father didn't even know about me because he'd been drafted into the Army and killed in a truck accident out in California. But Aunt Mel and I get along fine, with no complaints. I guess that's the way it should be.

Sara came to live with us just four months ago, when the county welfare agent was frantic to find a foster home for her, and our preacher told her to ask Aunt Mel for help. Aunt Mel would never turn down a request from the preacher.

At first I hated Sara. Then I just thought about how glad I'd be when she left. Aunt Mel said we should enjoy our companionship since we both were seventeen, but age was the only thing we had in common.

Sometimes I thought there were two Saras: the brash one who wore her sweaters and blouses a size too small and had every guy old enough to be grown out of pimples and pudginess chasing after her, and the silent one, who sneaked from the house at night when she thought no one was watching her. She'd vanish into the darkness with no more noise than a wisp of smoke.

I was jealous of her right from the start. I admit it. Aunt Mel says I'm not skinny, I'm gaunt, and gauntness runs in our family. But it's hard to be gaunt up against someone who is put together like Sara.

But I was tired of thinking about her, and I burrowed my head into my goose-down pillow, batting at the ends until it puffed around my face. I wadded the edge of the quilt into the warm place under my chin. In the distance I heard the soft hoot of an owl and vaguely wondered if I were the only one in town who heard it. There are some around these parts who swear that an owl's hoot after midnight means death for someone. I shuddered a little in my warm cocoon and fell asleep.

In the morning I staggered through the ritual of getting ready for school. As soon as I went downstairs and slid into my chair at the kitchen table, Aunt Mel said, "Mornin', Lauren." She strode across the room and slapped a plate of steaming scrambled eggs in front of me. I stared at the shiny white streamers that tangled with the yellow lumps and groaned.

"Aunt Mel, you know I don't like eggs."

"Every young person needs a certain number of eggs for good health, cholesterol or no cholesterol," she said as though that settled the matter forever. I suppose it did. Her rules were as tightly drawn as the gray hair she pulled up into a polished bun on the top of her head.

I reached for the plate of buttered toast, and my eyes met Sara's clear blue ones. Her slow smile was sugared cream, spilled from the smugness of knowing things I didn't know, being where I had never been and might never go.

Aunt Mel seated herself at the end of the long wooden table and looked from Sara to me and back to Sara, her head swiveling like the referee's at a tennis match. She cradled a steaming cup of tea in her long fingers.

"Beats me why you two girls can't be friends," she said.

I looked down at my plate and took a large mouthful of the eggs, trying not to taste them. I followed with a gulp of orange juice.

"Aunt Mel," I said, "I can't find my new bra— the white one. Did you see it when you did the wash?"

She thought a minute and nodded. "It might have got into Sara's dresser drawer by mistake."

Sara giggled. "If I find it, I'll be sure to return it to you, Lauren. It wouldn't do me any good. I outgrew that size when I was twelve!"

The toast was a brick wall, and I bit through it easily, chomping it to bits. I was ready to take on the walkway and gate next, but Aunt Mel interrupted.

"Watch your time," she said. "Y'all are running late."

"Does that mean I don't have to finish my eggs?" I asked.

"It means eat faster," she said.

Sara was already standing on the porch, looking bored, by the time I grabbed my books. I hurried out the door, and she kept pace with me. We walked for no more than half a block in silence, past Fant and Feenie Lester's tidy yard, and past the Swazes' clutter of tricycles and tennis shoes before Sara spoke.

"You know Roberta Campion?"

"Sure," I said.

Our school isn't so big that you don't know everyone in it. Roberta's family was new in town last year. They rented a house on its outskirts, but they didn't mingle with the townspeople. I should say that the people of the town didn't have much to do with the Campions because they're new and different, being part Cajun from over Louisiana way. In this part of East Texas, near the wild, dense forest and swamp area called the Big Thicket, everybody has known everybody forever, and most of them are related in some way. They don't take much to outsiders.

Roberta was a strange girl who kept to herself a lot. I didn't feel unfriendly, but I didn't know what to do with her.

11

"She's psychic," Sara said. "Bet you didn't know that."

"What's so special about that? Half the people in town can tell you when to plant beans, and if you're going to have unexpected company because you dropped a fork, or if it's going to rain because there's a ring around the moon."

"That's not the same thing," Sara said, lifting her nose and looking important. "Roberta can contact the dead."

I stumbled over a tree root that had broken through the sidewalk, caught my balance, and stopped in my tracks, staring at Sara. "She's crazy!" And out of spite I added, "So are you for believing that garbage!"

"The trouble with you, Lauren, is that you've spent all your life in this narrow little town and have no sophistication at all."

"Believing in that Halloween stuff is supposed to be sophistication?"

Sara tugged at my arm. "Come on. We'll be late, and Mrs. Dean will have my hide!"

The first bell rang as we reached the patch of lawn in front of the old brick building with its seal embedded over the door, like the eye of a Cyclops. We dashed up the wide steps and into our classrooms. For a while I tried to cram geometric rules and historical dates into my head, and I forgot all about my conversation with Sara.

Allie brought it up at lunchtime. We were at a stained Formica table in the corner of the large cafeteria, which has been painted a bile green for more years than anyone can remember. We were sharing her peanut-butter sandwiches because I'd forgotten my lunch. Allie leaned across the table and said, "This is confidential. Strictly between us. I heard from someone who swears that it's true that Roberta Campion can hold séances and contact the dead."

I sighed. Allie is my closest friend and always has been, just as she's always been round and short with a disposition like toasted marshmallows. She never varies, never changes. Except for her hair. It's either as limp as the hair on a wet brown cocker spaniel, or shocked into an electric charge of home-permanent frizzies. Today it was limp, and she kept twisting it around her fingers.

"Was that someone Sara Martin?" I asked her.

Allie's eyes and mouth widened at the same time. "How did you guess?" she asked. Then she blinked. "Oh, of course. You live in the same house with Sara. She'd certainly tell you."

"I don't believe all that stuff about Roberta."

Allie reached across the table and grabbed my arm. "We could try it," she said. "If Roberta has a séance, we could go."

"Go the hell where?" A tray was plopped down next to me, and I watched Maddie Cartney climb over the bench and sit down. Maddie was throwing a lot of "hells" and "damns" and a few other things into her talk, just to drive her mother up the wall, and it was getting to be such a habit she sometimes used the words when her mother wasn't anywhere around.

"To a séance," Allie said. "But don't tell anyone, because it's confidential."

"Sara didn't tell me it was a big secret," Maddie said.

For an instant Allie looked deflated as she watched Maddie spoon up her "beef surprise." Then she righted herself and said, "Are you going?"

"No one's said there's anything to go to," Maddie answered.

"But Roberta is going to get a bunch of people together and hold a séance," Allie said. She added, "At least I think she will."

I shook my head. "Can you imagine what the people in town would say if they knew there was going to be a séance? Aunt Mel would have a fit. And I bet a lot of parents would get mad enough to pop."

Maddie began to look interested. She sucked the last bit of the mixture from the end of her spoon and said, "All in all, going to a séance might be fun. If Roberta's going to have one, put me down for it."

"But your mother . . ." I began.

"Yeah," Maddie said with a smile. She stared into her plate. "I wonder what the hell I just ate."

"The usual offering from the poison pantry," I said. "Try not to think about it."

We broke up in giggles, getting a stern look

from the cafeteria monitor. Nothing more was said about the séance, and when I passed Roberta in the hallway, as I was going to my English class, she seemed so small and plain and nondescript I didn't give the séance a second thought. I remembered it later and wondered how a shy mouse like Roberta could have become involved with voices from another world. It didn't make sense.

I rounded a corner and bumped into a couple of the guys on the football team. They were leaning against the lockers, talking to Sara, hanging over her as though she were a double fudge sundae at half price. And she was gazing up at them from under heavy eyelids, her lips wet and slightly parted. None of them noticed me.

"Was it one of you?" I thought to myself. "Did Sara sneak out last night to meet one of you?" If I'd paid attention to the car that had pulled up in front of our house in the darkness, I might have known the answer.

I promised myself to wish on the next load of hay I saw that Sara would leave, would go somewhere else. Where? I didn't care. I just wanted Sara Martin out of my life!

2

I never walked home with Sara. Allie and I usually scuffed along the sidewalk, kicking at dead leaves, and turned toward either her house or Aunt Mel's. But today Allie stayed for band practice, and I went back home alone. Sara was about a block ahead of me, and I kept it that way. I didn't feel like talking to Sara any more than I had to.

It wasn't surprising when a car slid to the curb and the man in it leaned over to talk to Sara. Her body language could be read without any trouble as she hurried to the car and got in. What was surprising was that the man in the car was Sheriff Ashe Norvell.

Sara didn't show up again until time for supper, and then she was a few minutes late. Aunt

Mel, her eyes on the blueberry muffins she had just taken out of the oven, said, "Sara, things are getting cold."

"Sorry," Sara answered, pulling out her chair. "I had a project to work on at the school library. I had to stay late."

I stared across the table at Sara, and her blue eyes were as clear as unmuddied spring water.

"I noticed you talking to Sheriff Norvell today," I said, not dropping my gaze for a minute.

Aunt Mel put down her fork and leaned forward. "Whatever for?" she asked.

Sara didn't stop eating. "He just wanted to ask me about my birthdate," she said. "There was some mix-up on the records, and the county welfare agent asked him to find out."

Aunt Mel began to talk about the county welfare agent's cousin, who was thinking of moving to Oklahoma and going into the business of raising chickens. I tuned it out, so I was startled when Aunt Mel suddenly said, "Lauren, your mind's off skittering, and I just told you that I'm going to a meeting of the church ladies tonight."

"That's nice, Aunt Mel," I said. "Hope you have a good time." I got up to clear the table and scrape the dishes.

"You can lend Lauren a hand," Aunt Mel told Sara as she rose from her chair.

I knew that was the last thing Sara had in mind, and I was grateful that Aunt Mel knew it, too.

Sara nodded, as though something were bothering her, and picked up a couple of empty glasses.

"You're going to be in early, aren't you?" Sara asked Aunt Mel.

She chuckled. "Sounds as though you're the mother hen, and I'm the chick."

"I . . . I just meant . . ." It was the first time I had seen Sara flustered.

"Should be about ten, ten-thirty," Aunt Mel said. She flipped off her apron and hung it on a hook behind the door in one unbroken movement. "I'm running late," she said. "Got to pick up Feenie in a couple of minutes. Y'all take care now while I'm gone. Do your homework."

Quickly she gathered some of the muffins into a dish and put a paper napkin over it. "Going to take these to Feenie. She's a poor cook, and, bless Fant's heart, he deserves something tasty once in a while."

I laughed with Aunt Mel, and for a moment we were close, sharing a private family joke.

"Have a good time at your meeting," Sara said.

Aunt Mel checked all the doors, making sure they were locked. She'd done this ever since a drunk from the lumber camp staggered into Iva Jean Crater's kitchen and hit her on the head with a wooden basting spoon. Each time Aunt Mel locked the doors she muttered under her breath how in a small town you shouldn't have such worries. I never worried. As I recalled the story, Iva Jean recovered her wits enough to dump her whole pot of stew on the man, and they had to take him to the hospital down in Beaumont. Iva Jean got nothing out of it except a small bump on her forehead and a story that she told for two months solid to anyone who'd stand still long enough to listen.

When Aunt Mel had gone, Sara turned a glass around on her finger, rubbing the dish towel against the sides and watching it shine.

"This reminds me of when I was younger, with my mother," she said. "We'd work together in the kitchen, and we'd laugh, and she'd tell me little stories and sometimes sing to me."

"That would be nice," I said. Another world I'd never know.

"And sometimes my father would come in, too. It wasn't a very big kitchen, so we'd giggle and get in each other's way, and then my father would pick me up, and they'd hug and kiss me."

I could only nod. There was a tight place in my chest. I didn't mean to be jealous of Sara, and I was glad she had had such a wonderful family life, but every time I tried to picture myself in a situation like that, full of warmth and love, the pictures popped like bubble gum, and I was left with an even greater emptiness than before.

"Are you listening to me?" Sara said. "I was telling you about how my mother and father would take me to the zoo."

I let the dirty water run out of the sink, wiped my hands on the trailing end of the dish towel

Sara was holding, and shook my head. "Sara, why did you tell Aunt Mel that you were at the school library today? I saw you get in Sheriff Norvell's car with him and drive off."

Sara's eyes opened a little wider. "And you're going to tell Aunt Mel. Is that it?"

"No," I said. "I don't tell Aunt Mel anything about you." I walked out of the kitchen, went into the living room, dropped into a chair, and picked up a magazine.

Sara followed me, dish towel still in her hands.

"What do you mean . . . anything?" she demanded.

"You know what I mean."

Sara perched on the arm of the overstuffed chair. "No," she said quietly. "I can't imagine what you're talking about."

I shouldn't have let myself get so angry. I told myself later that it was dumb, that nothing Sara did or said should have made any difference to me. But at the moment I couldn't stand her prissiness, and I said, "Who do you think you're fooling, Sara? You think you can sneak in and out of the house without anyone's knowing about it?"

Sara slid down into the chair, dropping the towel on the floor. She smiled at me, and the smile was one of contempt. "Spying, are you? Hoping to find out what I've got that you wish you had?"

"Don't be stupid!" I yelled. "I wasn't spying on you!"

20

"Sure you were." She leaned forward. "Would you like me to tell you who I go out with and what we do? Would you want to know what it's like to be with a real man who buys you a drink and drives home with you under the arches of trees that make it so dark you can—"

"Shut up!" I screamed at her. I jumped to my feet.

But Sara was on her feet, too, facing me. "It's none of your business what I do or where I go!" she yelled. "And don't think you can snitch to Aunt Mel, because I'll deny it!"

"I told you that I have no intention of telling her!" I slammed the magazine against the wall. "Oh, why don't you get out of here? I wish you'd go away and never come back!"

Suddenly Sara's voice was as soft as kitten fur. "Why don't you go all the way and wish I were dead?" She smiled lazily.

The words seemed to hang in a little pool of quiet air as the remembered echoes of our shouts banged around the walls and faded away.

In the strange stillness I lowered my voice, too. "I'd never wish that on anyone," I said.

She was smiling, and her smile was almost one of delight.

"Why are you looking at me like that?" I asked her. "What's the matter with you?"

"I was just thinking about what you said." She giggled.

The way she was acting made me feel creepy.

21

"You're weird," I told her, and I went upstairs to my room to study. I had nothing more to say to Sara.

The murmur of her voice carried up the stairs. She was on the phone, probably canceling a late date. For a moment I wondered whom the date had been with. Then I told myself firmly that I didn't care.

Sara and I didn't talk to each other the next morning on the way to school, but at lunchtime, when Allie and I settled at our favorite table in the corner, Sara joined us.

"Everybody will be here in a few minutes," Sara said. She motioned an eager sophomore away from the table with an imperious wave of her hand that almost caused him to drop his tray.

"What's this all about?" I asked, swinging one leg over the bench.

Allie grabbed my arm. "Don't get up, Lauren. We're having a meeting."

"What kind of meeting?"

"About Roberta's séance!" Allie said.

"That's dumb."

"No. At least stay and listen," Allie said.

Sara just sat and watched me. I stared at her.

"Please stay," Sara said.

The word "please" stunned me so much I settled down again.

Luemma joined us, fishing dill pickles out of a plastic bag, and drawling through her nose, "This is the most exciting thing I've ever heard of!" She was getting strands of her long pale hair in with the dripping pickles, and I turned away, unable to watch.

Maddie and Dana plopped onto the bench, tucking their legs under the table. They had brought sack lunches, too. Dana's plump fingers spread out a paper napkin and dumped the contents of her sack on it: half a cheese sandwich and two carrot sticks. Dana was perpetually on a diet.

When Roberta arrived at the table, I don't know. Suddenly I realized she was sitting there, in the last place on the end, looking from one to the other of us with big owl eyes, blinking a bit, as though someone were going to tell her to leave.

"Hi, Roberta," I said. The others looked at her eagerly.

Her black hair was tied back on her neck with a blue ribbon. For the first time I noticed that her eyes were as black as her hair. She was really a beautiful girl. And yet she wasn't. What was there about Roberta that—?

Allie interrupted my thoughts by saying, "Well, Roberta? Tell us. Are we going to have a séance?"

"I've . . . I've only done it a few times," Roberta said, but her eyes had begun to spark, and her cheeks grew pink. "I mean, if you're really sure you want me to do this . . ."

"We're sure," Sara said, leaning toward her eagerly.

"Wait a minute," I said. "What are we getting into?"

"It's just for fun," Dana told me.

"What the hell," Maddie said.

I thought about Aunt Mel. "Listen, the adults in this town will have all kinds of a tizzy if they know about it."

"So we won't let them know," Luemma said.

"Have y'all talked about this before?" I asked. I looked at each in turn.

Allie was the only one with the grace to look embarrassed. "Well, we knew you'd have to be talked into it, Lauren." She shrugged. "But it's a game. It's just for fun. Lots of people do this."

Roberta sucked in her breath. "It's not a game, Allie."

Allie looked bewildered. "It's not?"

"I really can contact those who have gone beyond," Roberta whispered. It was noisy as usual in the cafeteria, but we all heard her.

"This is not something for children," Sara said. She looked right at me.

Allie answered. "We're not children."

Luemma wiped some pickle juice off her chin and spoke up. "We've all read about séances, and we've seen things about them in movies. Now's our chance to really be involved in one. I think it's exciting."

"It can't hurt us," Dana said. She glanced at Roberta. "Can it?"

"We simply contact the spirits," Roberta said. "We talk with them. We receive any messages they may want to send us. That's all there is to it."

24

Somehow Roberta seemed to have grown taller. She was sitting on the bench, back as straight as the little plastic Buddhas in the gift shop. Her hands were resting, palms up, in her lap, and her eyes were steady and calm. I got the feeling she was ready to have the séance at any moment, if we just asked her.

"I think we're all agreed that we want a séance," Sara said. "It's just a matter of choosing a time and place."

"I didn't say I was going along with this," I told her.

"Please come, Lauren," Allie said. "I know I'm going to be terrified, and I want you to be there."

"To protect you?" I laughed.

"Lauren's afraid to come," Sara said.

"Lauren wouldn't be afraid of a séance," Allie said, "especially since she doesn't believe in them."

Sara continued. "Lauren's afraid of something else. She's afraid her wish will come true."

"What wish?" Maddie asked.

I could feel my cheeks grow warm. Was it embarrassment or anger? I didn't know. "Obviously it means a great deal to you to have me there."

"Yes, it does," Sara said. I knew there was more coming, but I could see that Sara wasn't going to tell me her reasons then and there.

Perhaps curiosity got the best of me. I shrugged and said, "All right. I'll come."

The bell rang, and people began to get up from

their tables. Roberta leaned toward us quickly. "Friday night," she said. "The time of the full moon is the best time of all."

"Where will we meet?" Dana asked.

"At my house," Roberta said. "My parents are going to Houston overnight on business. We'll have the house to ourselves."

"Okay," Maddie said. "We'll be there."

Next to me I could feel Allie shudder. I knew how she felt. I was trying to remember what had been said, why I had found myself agreeing to go along with this. I didn't really want to go to a séance.

I stood up and found Sara across from me. Her eyes were still fastened on mine. That was my answer. I was really going to prove something to Sara . . . or was it to myself? Maybe she was right. Maybe I was hoping my wish would come true.

3

On Friday I set out for the séance with a queasy feeling in the pit of my stomach. It was a crooning kind of evening. A couple of sleepy doves were coaxing each other from the sweet gum trees, and in the distance a hound was lazily baying to a low-hanging moon that looked like a fat glob of butter. Sara and I scuffed up the red dust road that led to Roberta Campion's house. We both were nervous, and we jumped now and then at the tiny noises in the night. Aunt Melvamay would have had a fit if she'd known we were going to a séance.

"Is she going to get really mad?" Sara asked, as though she had tuned in on my thoughts.

"Probably," I said, "but she's a controlled kind of person and gets over things in a hurry."

"You know her a lot better than I do, Lauren," Sara said, which was an obvious statement to make—about what I'd expect from Sara. She hadn't realized who would suffer the consequences of what we were doing. Believe me, I'd thought about it.

Sara giggled nervously. "What do you think Roberta is going to do?"

"I don't know," I said, stubbornly trying to be obtuse. "I've never been to a séance before."

"I've read about them," Sara said. "They're scary, especially when the lights are out."

"What if Roberta doesn't turn out the lights?"

"She'll have to. Roberta's got to come up with something to scare us, or nobody's going to go along with those messages from the other world and all that stuff."

Sara went on talking, but I stopped listening. My mind was leaping in a dozen different directions at once.

We got to the small one-story frame house Roberta shared with her parents and picked our way across the dirt yard, where tired grass blades seemed to huddle together in scattered clumps as though seeking protection. I felt sorry for Roberta. None of us had paid much attention to her at school until she started talking about having psychic powers and being able to contact the dead. It didn't seem fair. Now, because we were excited about the séance, we were using her.

Just as Sara raised her hand to knock at the

front door, I said, "Are you sure you want to go through with this?"

"You know I do!" she said, her eyes sparking with a look I'd seen before but had never understood. "Don't back out now, Lauren! You can't!"

I shrugged, and before I could answer, the door opened. Roberta stood there with a deep, intense look on her face. She was dressed for the part she was going to play, and for a moment I wanted to laugh. Her jet-black hair was wound in braids like a crown around her head, and the heavy brown makeup around her eyes made them look as though they were floating freely on her face. She was draped in a huge black shawl, which covered her blouse, and she wore a long flowered skirt that looked as though it belonged to someone a couple of sizes larger. It created an eerie effect, and I decided, with a shiver, that it wasn't funny after all.

We followed Roberta into the living room, where Maddie, Luemma, Allie, and Dana were already seated on the floor. They all had the same expressions on their faces: a mixture of excitement and a little bit of fear. I knew how they felt. This séance was getting to me the same way.

"You're the last to arrive," Roberta said, and she looked at us so reproachfully that I found myself stammering an apology.

"Just sit in the circle, please," Roberta interrupted.

I quickly squeezed into the nearest place on the

floor between Allie and Luemma, but Sara calmly walked around the circle and sat next to Roberta.

The room was poorly furnished but clean, with bargain-basement matched upholstered furniture, a couple of Formica tables, and a plain floor lamp. Shades had been pulled over the windows at the front of the house, and though all of us were sitting in a tight circle on the living-room floor, the house had an empty feeling, as if it were hollow and no one were really there.

Luemma had the giggles, and Dana kept poking her, making her giggle all the more. Allie joined in, and soon we were all feeling silly. Except for Roberta. There was a scowl on her face. Suddenly she clapped her hands. "Quiet!" she shouted.

It jolted us into silence, and we sat there almost without moving. I could hear Luemma's raspy breathing and the drip of a water faucet somewhere in the house. Off in the distance I heard the hoot of an owl.

"Danger," I said, "even though it's before midnight."

"What?" Allie had jumped. "What are you talking about?" They all stared at me.

"The owl's hoot," I said. "Didn't y'all hear it?"

They just looked at me. No one answered.

"Well, I heard it," I said. "It was off a ways, but I heard it."

"Don't talk about it," Maddie said. "It's bad luck."

"If you'll be quiet, please," Roberta said very

formally, "we can get on with the preparations for the séance."

She carefully arranged a setting with a white candle in a plain glass candlestick next to a small vase of late-blooming periwinkles. We all watched the movement of her fingers as though we were hypnotized.

Allie, who had given herself another bad permanent, so that her brown hair frizzed out around her face, was wearing a heavy, sweet perfume, and I rubbed my nose with my knuckles, trying to push the smell away. In that close room it made me feel a little sick.

Roberta finished her arrangement and sat upright, her hands resting, palms up, on her crossed legs. She would have seemed the picture of calm repose, except that her hands were trembling.

"We have the flowers as a sign of beauty in nature to appease the spirits," she said. She looked carefully at each of us in the circle, her eyes lingering on my face. "I hope there are no skeptics here. One who does not believe can ruin it for everyone. The spirits will not come if they are mocked."

Luemma giggled nervously, but Roberta waited patiently until the room was again perfectly still. "We have a few rules," she said. I decided she was satisfied I wouldn't cause a problem. "We must be silent, and we must concentrate, so that we can provide the right atmosphere for the spirits.

When one of them speaks to us, you may ask it questions. It will speak through me."

"What kind of questions?" Allie asked.

"Anything within reason," Roberta said.

"Aren't you going to turn out the lights?" Sara asked.

Allie looked around nervously. "Are the doors locked? We're here alone, and it's dark outside, and . . . well, I just thought I'd ask if the doors are locked."

"They're locked," Roberta said.

"Are you sure?"

Roberta gave a long, pained sigh. "Why don't you go see for yourself? We'll wait until you get back."

Maddie shook her head. "This is taking too damn long," she said. "You check the back door, Allie, and I'll check the front door."

They scrambled to their feet and were back in a matter of seconds. In a way I knew how Allie felt. It was getting creepier in this place by the minute.

Allie, who had farther to go through the house, was breathing heavily as though she had been running. As she dropped down next to me, her arm brushed mine, and it was damp with sweat. Even through her cloying perfume I could smell the bitter odor of fear. Allie had been so insistent about coming. I don't think she knew how scared she would be.

For a long time we sat in total silence. There

was a scratching noise against the house that gave me shivers. It was probably a tree branch, but it sounded like something clawing to get inside.

Again there was the hoot of an owl, an urgent, mournful call. I could feel it along my backbone.

Dana shivered. "The owl!"

"Silence!" Roberta said.

Again we sat quietly. Roberta closed her eyes. The rest of us looked at one another as though hoping for a clue as to what we should do. Luemma kept pushing her long hair away from her face with little jerky motions, and Maddie chewed on her lower lip.

When Roberta spoke, we all jumped. Spirits or no spirits we were getting psyched out. Roberta's voice was low, and she seemed to stare at a spot directly over my head.

"We're ready to begin," she said. "Will someone please turn out the lamp when I light the candle?"

Sara's glance caught mine. She had that triumphant look of someone who's been proved right.

Roberta leaned over, struck a match, and lighted the candle. If her fingers were burned as the last of the matchstick curled black, she didn't show it. She seemed to be in a weird state of unawareness.

Luemma turned out the floor lamp. The flickering light from the candle crept up and down the faces in our circle, adding a glitter to everyone's eyes that made them look like the glass eyes in a

33

stuffed doll. Our shadows moved in spasms over the walls. Allie shuddered.

Roberta began to murmur to herself in a singsong voice, humming a little tuneless song. Soon she began to rock back and forth.

"We are together!" She spoke the words so suddenly that I gasped.

Roberta opened her eyes and looked at each one in the circle. "We must concentrate together," she said firmly. "If we are to reach into the unknown, we must go there together."

"Who are we going to reach?" Maddie whispered.

"We will call and see who answers the call," Roberta said. She closed her eyes again and began a small humming sound in the back of her throat.

When she spoke again, it was softly, as though she were having a private conversation with another person. "I am glad you came," she said. "What do you have to tell us?"

There was breathless silence in the room as Roberta said, "One of us has lost some money."

"Oh! That's me!" Allie said. "I did! I really did! I'm always losing things. And this was two dollars I was supposed to pay back to my brother and—"

"Silence," Roberta said, and Allie subsided into a tight knot of arms and legs.

"Consider your money lost forever," Roberta said. "It will never be found." She paused and added, "Someone here is having trouble with her boyfriend."

Luemma and Dana began to speak at once, looked at each other, and lowered their heads, giggling.

"Dana will receive a call from the one she wants to hear from," Roberta said in her strange low voice, as though she were reciting a shopping list.

"How soon?" Dana whispered, but Roberta ignored her and continued.

"Maddie will have an argument with her mother."

"Dammit, don't I always!" Maddie sighed.

I laughed aloud, and for a few moments Roberta was quiet, simply continuing the solemn rocking back and forth. There was a tightness in the air around me, a tense feeling as though I had angered someone or something by being unpardonably rude. I wondered if I should apologize, but it seemed better to remain silent. I didn't like the feeling that something besides us was present in the room. I was frightened and wished I hadn't let Aunt Mel think this was going to be just a get-together to play records and eat junk food.

"Do any of you have any questions? The spirits are here. They are listening to you," Roberta whispered. At first I wasn't sure it was Roberta. It sounded more like a bodyless voice drifting into the room.

I had the distinct feeling that something was watching me. It was so terrifying I felt my hands get damp, and my breath came in short gasps. I don't think I was the only one who felt it. A sense of fear in the room gripped us all.

I was ready to quit. No matter what I had promised in the beginning, now I just wanted out. I had my mouth open to tell them that this was the end, that we were fooling around with real danger, when Sara gave a little cry that froze me. I couldn't move.

"No!" Sara said. "There's something wrong here!"

Allie moved closer to me, and Roberta turned to stare at Sara.

"What's the matter?" Roberta whispered.

Sara began to shake. "There's something fearful in this room! There's something terrible! Don't you feel it?"

Dana let out a strangled gasp. "Don't do that, Sara! You're scaring me!"

Sara's voice grew louder, and she got up on her knees, her hands clawing the air. I was halfway up myself, trying to break loose from Allie's frantic grip, when Sara suddenly screamed a blood-curdling yell and fell forward on the candle, snuffing out the only light in the house.

We were all shrieking, grabbing for one another in the darkness. Someone was sobbing loudly. I got tangled up in the cord to the floor lamp and banged my shins against a table.

"Turn on the light!" Roberta was shouting over and over. The floor lamp was one of the first things I had knocked over, and no one seemed to be able to find it in the dark tangle of frightened bodies.

Finally, I crawled across the floor, getting my fingers stepped on, and groped for the candle and matches lying in a damp spot on the rug where the vase of flowers had tipped over. I quickly lit the candle, not bothering to look for its holder. Dana righted the floor lamp, found the plug that had been pulled from the socket when the lamp went over, and managed to plug it in and turn it on.

With the steady light in the room, the aura of mysticism vanished like the last of the bathwater down a drain. I blew out the candle and got to my feet.

"What happened?" Maddie asked. She had her arms around Allie, who was shaking like someone caught in a frozen-game locker. Maddie sounded angry. "Sara, what the devil made you act like that?"

No one answered.

We looked around. "Where's Sara?" I asked.

"Maybe she's in the bathroom. Maybe she ran outside," Dana said.

Luemma was at the front door. "She didn't go out this way," she said. "The dead bolt's still locked."

We spread out in that little house, and that wasn't hard to do. Sara wasn't anywhere, and the safety chain was still on the back door. The screens were on the windows, and they all hooked on the inside.

Roberta shook her head. "She couldn't just disappear."

I looked at her carefully, but the weird eye shadow masked the expression in her eyes, and I couldn't tell what she was thinking.

"What did you do, Roberta?" Allie asked. She began to cry again.

"I didn't do anything!" Roberta said. Her voice was trembling now, and we could tell that she was frightened, too. "Sara couldn't just disappear into the air!" she added. "It's not humanly possible."

"Are you telling us that something inhuman happened to Sara?" Maddie demanded.

"Don't say that." Allie moaned.

"Listen," I said, "we can't just stand here yelling at each other. We've got to face facts. Sara said there was something wrong here, and then she disappeared, and the doors and window screens are locked."

Maddie turned on me. "You too? Are you going to try to tell us that something inhuman took her away? You're crazy!"

"I'm saying those are the only facts we have."

"So what do we do about them?"

"There's just one thing left to do," Luemma told Maddie. "Somebody's got to call the sheriff."

Roberta sat down with a plop, as though her legs had given out. "Luemma is right." She sighed. "The phone's in the kitchen. Somebody please call the sheriff."

Dana left to make the call, and I sat there wishing I didn't have to try to explain what had happened to Aunt Melvamay. Nothing I could say would sound logical. Only Sara could tell us what happened.

"Oh, Sara," Maddie said with a stamp of exasperation. "Where in hell are you?"

That was when Allie fainted.

4

Maddie made the phone call while the rest of us brought Allie around. Maddie didn't tell Sheriff Norvell why we needed him. She just asked him to come. He apparently didn't think anything a bunch of teenaged girls could dream up would be important enough for him to bring along his deputy, so he came alone, lumbering into the house in an awkward, heavy way as though he were afraid he might step on one of us.

But Ashe Norvell has been sheriff around our town for as long as I can remember, and he has the authority that goes both with the job and with being a big man among big men, so it wasn't long before he had us lined up in a tidy row on the sofa and chair while he straddled a hard-backed chair from the kitchen, facing us.

"When y'all are talkin' at once, like you was doin'," he said slowly, "the thought just don't come through. Now settle down and we'll take this one at a time."

He kept giving quick, appraising looks in Roberta's direction, probably trying to figure her out. If she'd washed off the dark eye shadow, she would have looked as normal as the rest of us—if you can call looking like scared night rabbits, with their wide round eyes, looking normal.

Roberta spoke first. She tried to tell him about the séance and what had happened. He just listened and waited, and when the story had been told, he said, "You really believe in all them spooky things? You think somebody you was talkin' to rose up from the grave and swooped off with Sara Martin?"

Roberta blushed, and the pulse point in her neck throbbed so that we could all see it. "The spirits only talk to me," she mumbled. "They don't materialize."

"You believe this?"

What could she say? She had worked up this spiritualism around herself as a way to get friends. Every one of us knew it deep inside, even though we had wanted to go along with the game. And it was a game. Wasn't it? The group just hadn't known how it would turn out.

Maybe the bug-on-a-pin thing works with the criminals Sheriff Norvell catches, but we weren't criminals, and I couldn't stand to see Roberta squirm. It wasn't fair.

"We were all here, not just Roberta," I said. "We heard what Sara said, and we saw what she did, and when we managed to get some light in the room again, that's when we found out that Sara was gone."

"None of y'all left the room?" he asked.

Maddie shook her head. "We would have seen if someone left."

"With the lights out?"

"But . . ." Her voice faded out, and we all looked at each other.

"Let me put it this way," the sheriff said. "Did any of y'all leave the room while the lights were out?"

None of us answered.

"Maybe it's some funny trick y'all hatched up together," he said. "After everyone in town gets all excited, y'all will come up with the answer to the riddle and have a big laugh at our expense. I know how kids think."

"Dammit! We're not kids," Maddie said indignantly. "We're seniors in high school. We called you because we don't know what happened, and we're upset about it."

Allie sniffled. "I want to go home. If you're not going to believe us, then I just want to go home."

"Calm down," he answered. He shifted his weight, and the chair wobbled. "I need some questions answered." He turned to me. "Lauren, fill me in on Sara. Y'all live in the same house. What's she like?"

I took a deep breath. "I don't know much about Sara. We weren't—aren't very good friends."

"Why not?"

"Because . . . well, we're just too different."

I stopped, and he said, "Keep goin'. You haven't told me much of anythin' yet except that you don't like Sara. Why not?"

What could I say? That I didn't like her because I wished I looked like Sara so that somebody would love me? I didn't even know how badly I had always wanted to be held and loved and caressed until Sara came and drew those feelings from the air and laid them out in front of me like a newly frosted cake that couldn't be touched. Sara's whole body spoke of loving, and I knew that's what she sneaked out of the house for on the dark nights when she thought Aunt Mel and I were asleep.

I don't remember Aunt Mel ever hugging or kissing me, and I wished so hard that she had. All the hunger I ever had for the touching I had never known boiled up in me like a festering sore because I wasn't like Sara. I didn't have parents like the ones she'd once had, who had given her the love she told me about. And I couldn't gather boys around me to touch my shoulder, to nuzzle my hair, to—

Allie loyally stepped in. "Sara was a tramp," she said.

"She chased the boys?"

"Yes," Allie said.

"And the rest of y'all don't?"

"Not like Sara did!" Allie was incensed.

"So now you're tellin' me somethin' I should know," Sheriff Norvell said. "Sara was after the boys. Any particular one?"

We looked at each other again. No one answered.

"Lauren? You should know if anyone should."

"None of the guys came around the house. Sara used to talk to them at the drugstore and at school and . . . well . . . places like that."

"Melvamay didn't like the boys coming over to the house?"

I shrugged. "I don't know. I don't think it ever came up. It's just sort of a thing that worked out that way."

He nodded, thinking it over. "This much y'all have told me. How about what y'haven't told me?"

I shivered. Aunt Mel would have said somebody was walking over my grave, but it was just that Sheriff Norvell terrified me. Was he reading my mind? How did I know I could trust him?

"Well?"

I nodded. "I haven't told this to anyone—not even to Allie."

"Go on."

It was hard to get the words out. I concentrated by staring at the sheriff's hands, which he had clasped in front of him. They were shaped like blocks, big and solid and square, with dark hair matted on the backs. The knuckles were distended like punctuation marks along his fingers. They were powerful hands, and I wondered if he had ever had to kill anyone with them.

"Sometimes," I began slowly, "Sara went outside the house at night."

"Alone?"

"Yes. She thought that Aunt Mel and I were asleep, I'm pretty sure, or she wouldn't have gone because she never said anything about going or made any excuses the next morning."

"How long did she stay out? All night?"

"No," I said.

"How do you know this?"

I could feel everyone staring at me, and my face burned. My eyelids were hot and raw. "Because a couple of times I waited at the window to see when she'd get back."

"Did you ever see anyone with her?"

"No. She always came back alone, the way she left, so quiet and quick-moving in the dark that I'd wonder if I had seen her at all or if it was my imagination."

"Was it ever your imagination?"

His gaze was so sharp that I cried out, "No! You asked me to tell you about Sara, and I told you something I'd kept to myself, and now you're acting as though I were lying!"

"I don't think you're lyin'. In fact, I'm won-

45

derin' if she left tonight to meet someone."

"Who?" Dana blurted out.

"It might help if we knew," the sheriff said.

"I don't know how." Maddie twisted in her chair, tucking her feet up under her. "There weren't any guys around here tonight—just the seven of us."

"Until Sara disappeared, and that made six," Allie offered.

"And I don't think it makes a damn bit of difference what Sara was like or what she did late at night. The fact is that she isn't here, and that's why we called you," Maddie said.

"We don't know anything more now than we did in the beginning." Luemma sighed.

"I think we do," Sheriff Norvell said.

We all leaned forward a little. I found myself clutching the prickly plush arm of the sofa, rubbing, rubbing against the grain.

"I think Sara pulled a disappearin' act for reasons of her own," he said. "What they are, I don't know. She may turn up in an hour or so, and y'all will feel like a pack of fools for takin' it all so serious."

"What if she doesn't turn up?" I was surprised to find I was whispering.

"Then we'll have to find out who locked the door behind Sara," he said. "One of y'all had to be involved in her leavin' in order to have both the doors fastened behind her."

"But that means one of us would know what happened," Allie said.

"That's right."

We looked at each other, but at the same time we were really afraid our eyes would meet, so our glances shot back and forth from each other's faces like ricocheting bullets, leaving only little dents of mistrust.

"Go home now," Sheriff Norvell said. "Come tomorrow I may want to know the answer."

"We don't have the answer," Allie wailed.

"One of y'all does," he said. "Sleep on it."

The sheriff piled us into his big sedan. None of us offered to stay with Roberta, and guilt was thicker in the car than the bitter, stale cigar smoke that drifted from the open ashtray. One by one he dropped us off at our homes. He saved me for last, and he came up the walkway and into the house with me to face Aunt Melvamay.

Aunt Mel had been knitting and watching TV at the same time. It isn't in her to keep still for long. She took one look at us and said, "Where's Sara?"

I sat in the chair opposite her. The sheriff sat across from us on the flowered chintz sofa, the printed Peace roses shifting and stretching under his weight.

"It's like this, Aunt Mel," I said. "Sara and I didn't go to a party, the way I led you to believe. We went to a séance."

Her hands flew up to her cheeks, and she stared

at me through a picket fence of long, bony fingers. "You didn't! You wouldn't!" she said. "You know how I feel about your getting mixed up with the tools of the devil!"

"But it wasn't like that, really," I said. "It was just at Roberta Campion's house, and she was putting on a lot. It was sort of like a game of scaring ourselves."

"It's not a game," she answered. "There's things that don't bear fooling around with." She put her hands in her lap in two tidy piles, the way she'd put clean pillowcases into the cupboard. She looked straight at the sheriff and then at me, took a deep breath to steady herself, and asked, "But there's something more to be told. Isn't there? You still haven't told me where Sara is."

"I'm getting to that part," I said. "Sara began acting strange and yelling that there was something terrible in the room, and she fell on the candle and put it out."

"And?" She didn't let me pause for breath.

"And that's all we know about what happened. When we managed to get a candle lit again, and the lamp put upright and plugged in . . . well . . . Sara was gone. We looked all over for her, but she was gone."

"You mean she ran out of the house?"

I shook my head. "The doors were locked—one with a dead bolt and one with a safety chain—and all the screens on the windows were hooked on the inside."

48

"That's impossible!" Aunt Mel stood up and walked with the long manlike strides she takes from one end of the room to the other. She faced the sheriff. "Ashe, you know as well as I do that things from the other world aren't to be tampered with, but you also know that girls don't just get spirited away from a séance, no matter how foolish they're behaving."

"That's right," he said. He leaned back, stretched his legs, and took out a cigar. "Mind if I smoke?"

"I certainly do," she said. "Put that back in your pocket, and wait until you get home to pollute your own air."

"You always had a sharp tongue, Mel," he said, but he did as he was told.

"And I've got a sharp mind, too," she said. "I know when my leg's being pulled." She sat on the arm of my chair, and for a moment I thought she was going to put an arm around me, but instead, she straightened. "Lauren," she told me, "we've always got on well, you and I. I've always trusted you, and I think I've given you no cause not to trust me. Now, will you please explain to me what really went on?"

I couldn't take it any longer. I bent over, with my face in her lap, and wept all the tears I'd been saving up for years. I think that surprised her more than anything else that had happened because she didn't move until I had lapsed into hiccuping sobs. Then she held my face between her two hands and lifted it until I looked directly into her eyes.

"Were you crying about what happened to Sara?" she asked.

"No," I said honestly. "I was crying because I don't care what happened to Sara."

"Do you know?"

"No," I said.

"I believe you," she told me.

Aunt Mel got up and walked over to sit beside the sheriff. "Ashe, let's leave those locked doors out of our thinking. They're standing right in the middle of the question. It seems to me that the girl ran away, and the séance thing was to get everyone so confused they'd get sidetracked enough to give her a head start. The real question is: Did she go alone, or did she go with someone?"

"Y'all know of anyone she could have gone with?"

She shook her head. "No. Sorry to say, I don't. But I do recognize a few things, Ashe, and one is that girl had a bit of the jezebel in her."

He gave her a sudden look of surprise, then said, "Lauren told me that she'd seen Sara slip out of the house at night."

"You didn't tell me that, Lauren," she accused.

"Would you want me to tell tales?"

"She was in my care. I should have known what was going on, and you know I sleep hard." Then she sighed. "No, you've never been one to run to a body with a story to tell about someone else."

50

"The thing we got to do is decide on the next step," the sheriff said.

"It's already been decided," Aunt Mel told him. "There's nothing we can do until morning unless you want to put out a missing persons bulletin, which strikes me as a good idea, because I don't think Sara plans to come back. I doubt she went to Houston to join her mother, although you'll have to call her mother, of course."

I interrupted. "Sara has a mother? Then why wasn't she living with her mother?"

"She couldn't," Aunt Mel said. "Sara was a ward of the court."

"But why—"

She interrupted me this time, and I saved the question for later. Aunt Mel had her mind on one track now, and she was concentrating on that single direction.

"Tomorrow," she said to the sheriff, "you might check around and see if any of the boys in town who have more hot blood than brains are missing, too. I'd invite you for a cup of coffee, but I know you'd rather be outside where you can choke on that stinking cigar, so good night, Ashe."

"Mel," he said, shaking his head, "since I'm the sheriff around here, don't you think it would be becomin' of you to let me make the decisions?"

"So? What's your decision?"

He gave an elaborate sigh, then grinned, exposing large yellowed teeth. "About the same as yours, I reckon. Good night, Mel."

Sheriff Norvell hoisted himself to his feet, leaving the printed roses shuddering and sunken behind him. Aunt Mel walked with him to the front door, where they murmured a few things to each other before she returned to me.

I suppose I expected her to question me further, but she simply said, "Let's go to bed, Lauren. It's late. We'll think a lot better in the morning."

"Good night, Aunt Mel," I said. I went upstairs and left her to putter through her comforting ritual of closing drapes and locking doors and turning off the lamps, one by one.

It took me a long time to get to sleep.

By the next day the whole town knew what had happened. There are no secrets in a place like this. East Texans are a superstitious lot, each family with its own preternatural tales from the Big Thicket heritage of ghosts seen and believed, and strange lights from the swamps, and some relative or another who went into the Thicket never to be heard from again. It wasn't surprising that as many people believed Sara Martin had disappeared from the Campion living room, right into the air, as believed that something plausible had happened to her, especially since the Campions are part Cajun. That seemed to give some people the final proof that Roberta knew about spirit doings the rest of us could only guess at. It was the first time the Campions had been granted any respect since they arrived in these parts.

A couple of the ladies from Aunt Mel's church circle came by to offer their support, bringing some fresh-baked cinnamon buns, and to pump for all the details.

"I've heard of some strange things in this town," Iva Jean Crater said, "but I never heard of anyone having a séance. Whatever possessed you girls to try a thing like that?"

Mabel Kellock, who had squeezed in next to Iva Jean on the sofa, jostled her elbow so hard that the tea in both their cups sloshed into their saucers. "That's an unfortunate word to use," she said. She pointedly glanced upward.

Both ladies stared at me with suspicion in their eyes. Iva Jean crossed her fingers, putting her middle finger over her index finger. She thought her hand was hidden by her full skirt, but I saw the movement. She was protecting herself against me. I suddenly shivered as though a cold finger had traced my backbone.

Aunt Mel saw Iva Jean's gesture, too. She doesn't miss much. "The girls thought it was a game," she said. "They went into it just for the fun of it. Have another cinnamon roll, Iva Jean."

Iva Jean had already made great inroads into the cinnamon rolls she had brought, but she absentmindedly took another.

"I would bet those girls know something," Mabel Kellock said. She pursed her little mouth and tucked her head down into pink folds of neck so that she looked like a grouper fish, wary of the bait.

"Maybe if you started at the beginning and told us all about it, we'd discover something overlooked that would solve the whole disappearance," Iva Jean said. Her eyes glittered with eagerness.

"She's gone over it enough," Aunt Mel said brusquely. "Right now Lauren hasn't got time to sit around chatting. She's got things to do."

Aunt Mel sent me down to Granby's Food Mart to pick up some things for Saturday supper, and I couldn't help looking around at the people I passed on the street and the people in the crowded store. Most of them I recognized; a lot of them were acquaintances. It was funny that Aunt Mel had told Sheriff Norvell to look around for a missing boy, to find out if Sara had gone off with anyone. Aunt Mel was almost always right, of course, but what if the person Sara had met wasn't a boy? He could just as easily have been an older man. I tried my best to think of what Sara may have said about her likes and dislikes, and I came up with zero. I think I tuned her out when I should have tuned her in. But something told me the person Sara met didn't have to be as young as she was. Aunt Mel said we'd know who he was before long, when word got around that someone else was missing, too. I was really curious.

The Food Mart delicatessen sent out pungent odors of roasted brisket and sliced onions and hot fat from the fried chicken piled under the mustard-yellow heat lamps that kept them warm. I leaned against the shelves that held the boxes of cereal, forgetting my shopping for the moment as I tried to think of the men and boys I had seen Sara talking to.

There were Billy Stoner and Jim Billings from school. She was with Jim Billings a lot until she met Carley Hughes, and then she let Jim go like an undersized trout. I didn't blame her. Carley Hughes is a great-looking guy—tall, redheaded, a senior, and the big man in school in baseball. Without Carley Hughes our team wouldn't have won the state's championship. We'd never won it before in all the school's history, but Carley was something else, and we knew he'd get a scholarship offer from any university in the state. I wasn't the only girl who wished Carley would look at me the way he looked at Sara.

And there was Fant Lester, our next-door neighbor. Fant is probably thirty-five or so, and he's married to Feenie. They're a funny couple because they look so much alike. Feenie wears her hair short, like Fant's, and no makeup, and they go hunting together in their pickup truck for fun and even do the dishes and wash the clothes together. A lot of the men in town make fun of Fant for doing women's work, but it doesn't seem to bother Fant, as long as he's doing it with Feenie. And yet, I'd seen Sara beeline it over to Fant's backyard when he was outside working. She made it obvious that she thought he was attractive.

"Hello, Lauren," a deep voice said.

I shifted my weight and grabbed a box of Frosted Krinkles that was about to go over. I looked up into the perpetually sunburned face of Sheriff Norvell's deputy, Jep Jackson, and managed to stammer something, sounding like a total idiot. I had always thought Jep was the handsomest man in our town, and the story about him was romantic, too. Even though Jep is twenty-eight or so, he's never married. I've heard of how his sweetheart at Sam Houston University, down in Huntsville, ran off with someone else. Jep finished his second year in police administration, then came back here to the town where he was born and grew up. His hair is the same color as his skin, and unless he's in church or the market, when he's off duty, you never see Jep without his hound and his hunting rifle.

I wasn't the only one who thought Jep was something special. Sara did, too. That's one of the few things she did tell me, that day she heard me confide in Allie that I liked Jep. And it was the next day that she waved to me from his pickup truck as he drove her home from school. I remember because I was so jealous it hurt.

I looked up at him and thought with a sigh of relief, "It wasn't you, Jep. You're here, so it couldn't have been you she went away with."

"What's with you, Lauren?" Jep asked. "I say hello, and you stare at me like I came down with spots." He grinned.

"Sorry, Jep," I said. "I had my mind on Sara. I keep trying to think about . . ."

He waited for me to finish the sentence, but I couldn't. I didn't want him to know where my thoughts had taken me. So I quickly said, trying to cover up, "What has the sheriff done about Sara?"

"He put out an all-points bulletin," Jep said. "No one's seen her on any of the highways. All we can figure is that she hitched a ride, made it over to the highway, and is long gone from here."

I nodded. "This town had nothing for her, Jep."

"She had a place to stay here, and remember—she was underage."

"In her mind she wasn't."

"You think age is just a matter of what you want it to be?"

"With some people, maybe it is. I think Sara was one of those people."

"You ought to take psychology when you get to college," Jep teased. "You are going to college, aren't you?"

He had hit a sore point, and I winced. "I want to," I told him. "I want it more than anything I can think of, but I know Aunt Mel hasn't got the money, and I'd have to go off to the city and pay board. My grades aren't that good, so there's no way I can get a scholarship."

"What's the matter with the grades? Don't you like to study?" Jep grinned.

I tried not to blush, and was angry at myself

when my cheeks grew hot. "I suppose I could work harder, but if I can't afford to go to college anyway, A-grades aren't worth much. Are they?"

"All you're given me is arguments against," he said. "How about coming up with some arguments for?"

"Well—" I began, but just then there was a commotion at the door, and when Jep and I stuck our head around the counter, we saw Sheriff Norvell bearing down on us like an eighteen-wheeler.

"Jep!" he growled, a scowl on his face. "Come with me! Quick!"

"What's up?" Jep asked.

"Sara Martin," the sheriff said. "A hunter drove in from the Thicket a few minutes ago. He's got Sara's body in the back of his pickup!"

5

I left my basket in the aisle as I raced out of the store after Jep. But the two men were in the sheriff's car, tires kicking up spurts of gravel that slapped against the legs of my jeans. They'd gone without paying attention to my pleas to go along.

When it finally dawned on me that Mrs. McAndrews was tugging at my arm and telling me I should come inside and sit down, I realized that I had been standing in the street, making little whimpering noises like a hurt retriever pup.

"Come with me, Lauren," she said. "Sit down."

"No," I said. "I can't, Mrs. McAndrews. I've got to go home and tell Aunt Mel."

"Tell her what?" she asked. Her eyes were bright, and I could see beyond her to a dozen or so people who were standing on the sidewalk, listing toward me in an effort to scoop up the news I'd impart.

Oh, well. They'd know sooner or later, and telling them would be part of my penance. "A hunter found Sara Martin's body in the Thicket," I said carefully, spacing out the words. "He brought her into town."

They all started talking to one another at the same time, and I headed home. I realized later that I must have been walking like a zombie, repeating my message like a parrot to anyone I met who looked at me with concern.

Dana shrieked when I told her. She leaned against the wall of Snyder's drugstore and just stared at me with her mouth open.

Fant and Feenie Lester were coming out of the sporting-goods store when I told them. Feenie swore a little under her breath, but Fant closed his eyes for a moment, and when he opened them, I knew he had been thinking of something he'd never tell Feenie.

My mind wasn't registering. I should have been more aware of whom I was talking to and what I was saying. I bumped into Carley Hughes and a couple of his friends as I rounded the corner on Acorn Street and repeated my horrific news.

Carley turned white, and I mean really. I've read about people turning pale at bad news, but here it was in the flesh. He swayed the way pines do in a storm blown in from the Gulf, then grabbed my shoulder to steady himself. It was then I realized that Carley and Sara had been together a lot at school, and maybe he had been the one she'd been meeting lately after dark.

"I'm sorry, Carley," I said.

He just shook his head as though to clear it, turned around abruptly, and took off at a lope.

"He liked her, you know," one of the guys said. They stood there as though wondering what to do next, and I kept walking. I was never so glad to reach Aunt Mel's house.

She was in the kitchen, humming in an off key and stacking pans neatly one inside the other. She looked at me, then did a double take. "Lauren? What is it?"

I tried to pull myself together and be more gentle this time. "I was talking to Jep," I said, "and Sheriff Norvell came for him on the run. He said that a hunter had come in from the Thicket."

I stopped. Aunt Mel, never taking her eyes from me, led me to a kitchen chair and scraped another across the linoleum to face me.

"It's about Sara, isn't it?"

"Yes," I said.

She sighed. "You'd better tell me what you know, Lauren."

"I don't know much. Only that the hunter found Sara's body in the Thicket."

Aunt Mel's breath came out in little shuddering gasps. "How could it happen?"

I started to answer, then realized she was talking to herself. She shook her head back and forth

61

and looked a million years older than she had when I walked in the door. Slowly she stood and peeled off her apron, laying it across the back of the chair.

"I'll go down to Ashe's office," she said.

I stood, too. "I'll go with you."

"No," she said. "If the body's been in the Thicket, there's no telling what the animals and—" She stopped and shuddered. "You stay here," she said.

"I didn't get the groceries." I suddenly remembered.

"No mind." To my surprise she reached over and patted my shoulder, turned, and left the kitchen. I heard the front door of the house close gently, and I was left alone with my thoughts.

They weren't pleasant thoughts. I kept trying to figure out how a thing like that could happen to Sara. Had she wandered into the Thicket accidentally? How did she get there? And how did she die? Nothing made sense, but I could picture the dark tangle of pines and myrtles and oaks that kept the Big Thicket dim on even the brightest day. And the dense tangle of undergrowth, knotted together with tievines and briars. And the water moccasins that slip through ponds of swamp water, leaving silent ripples in their wake. And the rattlers, and the grunting wild hogs that attack the hunters and try to rip them apart with their tusks before the blast of a shotgun. There are people who love the Thicket and go there for the rich earth smells, and to gather mayhaws for jelly, but to me it's a fearsome place. I couldn't bear the thought of Sara's going inside the Thicket. What was she doing there? Why did she go?

It took a while to get some of the answers, and they weren't complete. Allie—her head bristling with huge pink rollers—came over as soon as she heard the news, and we were glad to have each other for company. Aunt Mel came back, still with her grayed look, blaming herself because Sara had been in her care, and she told us that some official had driven over from Beaumont and performed an autopsy and said that Sara had died by drowning.

"In the swamp?" I asked.

"She was found face down in the water."

"Was she . . . ? I mean, did some man. . . ?" Allie looked sideways at Aunt Mel, unable to finish her question.

"No," Aunt Mel said, staring at something outside the window. "She wasn't raped."

"I don't understand how she got into the Thicket," Allie said.

"She wasn't far from the road. She may have wandered into the Thicket and got lost. Plenty of people have been lost in the Thicket and never heard from again. Even their bodies haven't been found. At least they found Sara's."

Allie looked at Aunt Mel pleadingly, as though begging her for a satisfying answer. "Sara was in

Roberta Campion's living room with the rest of us," she said. "How did she get to the Big Thicket?"

"Someone knew she was leaving," I said. "Someone locked the door behind her."

Allie swiveled in my direction, hands fluttering. "Who did this, Lauren?"

"That's what Sheriff Norvell asked us," I said.

"It doesn't make sense. Was she running away?"

"I should have kept a sharper eye on the girl," Aunt Mel said. "After all, she was in my care."

"If the person who knew Sara was leaving the séance doesn't speak up, then all of us who were there are to blame," Allie said.

We sat there silently, wrapped in our individual shrouds of guilt, until Aunt Mel said, "Ashe phoned Sara's mother. She's coming up here, and I said she could stay at our house if she likes."

"Why wasn't Sara living with her mother?" I had to ask the question again.

Aunt Mel nodded, as though it wouldn't matter now who knew the story, and said, "Apparently, from what that social worker in Barnard told me when Sara came here to live, the girl was too much for her mother to handle, and they never got along well. Mrs. Martin finally had her daughter made a ward of the court. Then she went down to Houston to find work and is a barmaid at one of the downtown clubs. They couldn't find anyone in Barnard to take Sara, and since we're in the same county, they brought her here."

Sara had told me about her loving mother and father, and I had believed her. I had envied her. I had wanted that kind of love with all my heart and pined and ached because I could never live my childhood over and could never have it. It was one reason why I had hated Sara. Now I had to re-think it all. Maybe it was true when Sara had been little. Maybe she made it up. Maybe it was her own desperate wish, so she could have something to cling to after her mother gave her away. *"Oh, Sara,"* I thought, *"there was so much I didn't know about you, so much I wish we had talked about."*

We made some tea and stirred in honey and lemon and cinnamon to make the drink Aunt Mel calls her tranquillity tea. The three of us sat with our hands cupped around the hot mugs, sipping and letting the mental aches slip away.

When we heard heavy footsteps on the front porch and the jangle of the doorbell, I wasn't surprised. I put down what was left of my tranquillity tea and went to the door. Sheriff Ashe and Jep were there, and I escorted them in.

Aunt Mel was more her old self now, and she took charge. "How about a mug of my tranquillity tea?" she asked. "There's plenty for all."

Jep perked up and looked interested, but when he heard a recitation of the ingredients, he shook his head. "Naw. I thought there might be something else in there."

"If you mean spirits, then shame on you," Aunt

Mel said. She motioned to the unoccupied kitchen chairs, and the men sat down.

"Do y'all know how Sara's accident happened?'" Allie asked them.

"Accident?" Sheriff Norvell asked.

Allie got that little crease between her eyes that comes when she's puzzled. "You know," she said. "Sara Martin's accidental drowning?"

"You think it was an accident, do you?"

"Well, but what else—?" I interrupted, then stopped. I could see it coming.

"There's no way to prove it right now," he said, "and little to go on, but I got a hunch, and my hunches are usually right."

He pulled a cigar from his shirt pocket, took one look at Aunt Mel, and stuffed the cigar back. "I got a strong feelin' about Sara Martin's death," he said. "If y'all ask me, I think she was murdered."

I leaned back in my chair and gripped my mug of tea tightly. I had let them guess about what Sara was doing. I hadn't spoken up. I knew for a fact that Sara was meeting some man, was leaving town with him. That much she had told me, but who the man was I didn't know. And Sara had made me promise not to tell.

Sara hadn't talked of marriage. She had talked only of love. It could even have been a married man she thought she was running away with.

It wasn't hard to take a mental step forward. This man—whoever he was—hadn't gone away with her. Maybe he never intended to do so. But he let her think he would, and then . . . then he killed her.

I looked at Sheriff Norvell. I looked at Jep. I should tell them the rest of the story. Except . . . something held me back. I had no idea who the man was that Sara was going to meet. It could just as easily have been either of these two. And if I told what I knew, the murderer might think I knew even more.

I didn't want to be next on his list!

6

All night, as I dozed into and out of sleep, I kept telling myself that Sheriff Norvell had to be wrong. He was making too big a thing of it. Sara was supposed to meet someone, but she didn't tell me where. It was probably out of town aways, and she hitched a ride to that spot. Maybe she wandered into the Thicket. Maybe . . .

I knew better than that. Nobody would wander into the Thicket at night. Nobody would wait for someone on that stretch of highway. But who was the man who took her there? Sara wasn't close to any of us at school. If she had told anyone his name, it probably would have been me. And she hadn't.

Maybe the murderer was thinking along the same lines. Maybe he had come to my name and stopped. He would have no way of knowing that Sara had never even hinted at his name. I was cold in spite of the September heat that carried the scent of fresh-cut grass from the Lester house next door and the buzz of angry black bees diving in and out of clusters of fat yellow blossoms on the bignonia vine.

I hadn't wanted to go to church services Sunday morning, but Aunt Mel wouldn't hear of my staying home. I knew what would happen, and it did. Everybody from all around came to church because they knew our preacher would get going on the evils and dangers of devil worship and witchcraft and especially séances.

Luemma, Allie, Dana, and I had to sit there and take it, while people around us nodded in agreement, looked wise, and tossed us little skin-pricking glances filled with scandalized indignation and deep suspicion. Maddie got to stay home with monthly cramps, and Roberta's family attends church in the next town, so they lucked out.

I didn't expect sympathy from any quarter, even Aunt Mel, so I was surprised when, afterward, as we stood in the thick carpet of Saint Augustine grass at the door of the church, Ila Hughes, Carley's grandmother, stopped to talk to us.

"I'm sorry," she said, curling her fingers around my arm. "This is a hard thing for you girls to go through, especially hard for you, Lauren, since you and Sara shared a roof together."

69

I didn't know what to say, so I just nodded.

She turned to Aunt Mel. "I wouldn't put too much blame on the girls," she said. "There are a lot of folks around here who lay it to the dark side of things."

"Humph!" Aunt Mel said. "There's no point in getting wrapped up in superstitions, Ila."

"I'm not talking about superstitions," Mrs. Hughes said, poking her nose practically into Aunt Mel's face and peering at her over the top of her glasses. "I'm talking about facts we all know about. Like Tom Hawkins, who saw the ghost light in the swamps at least three times, and set off to track it, and disappeared altogether—not a trace of him left."

"He went too far into the Thicket," Aunt Mel said. "He got lost. It's as simple as that."

Mrs. Granbery, from over near the crossroads, had come to join us, and she shook her head so vigorously that her plump jowls shook. "Don't say you can put a reason to everything, Melvamay," she told my aunt. "I doubt but every family hereabouts has at least one kinfolk who had something mysterious happen to him in the Thicket."

"Mysterious only in that they disappeared or thought they saw something queer, or scared themselves witless," Aunt Mel said. She seemed to grow an inch taller.

"There are things that happen to people who fool around with spirits and demons and the like,"

70

Mrs. Granbery said. She gave me such a sharp look that I took a step backward.

But Mrs. Hughes patted my arm. "Don't blame these little girls if they were used unwittingly by the dark powers. All of us have done some fool things when we were young." Her lips turned up in a tremulous smile.

I tried to smile back.

"Y'all come to see me some afternoon," she said to me. "Between the lunch and dinner shift I'm usually home, picking up, doing the things that need taking care of. I'd like to talk with you."

"Thanks," I said.

I was ready to snap up gratefully any friendly gesture, but I did wonder about Ila Hughes. I knew she was raising her only grandson, Carley, and had since his parents had been killed in the lumber mill accident about ten years ago. She was working as a waitress to support the two of them. Rumor had it she was very frugal, and every extra cent she made went toward Carley's future college education. Carley worked part-time for it, too, and with the scholarship he was going to win, it looked as though he'd get those four years and come out with a degree.

"And a better life in the city," Mrs. Hughes would tell people. She wanted something more for Carley than he could get in our small town, where the main source of entertainment for the local men was hunting and fishing and sitting around Slade Snyder's drugstore, swapping lies.

71

On the walk home I said, "That sermon was rough, Aunt Mel."

"Did you deserve better?"

"No," I admitted.

She looked satisfied, and we walked without speaking for a few moments, concentrating on picking our way over the chunks of cement and tangled tree roots that had shattered the sidewalk in front of the old Noonan place on the corner.

"What did Ila Hughes do when she was young?" I asked.

Aunt Mel looked at me sharply. "What do you mean, what did she do? She went to school. She worked hard."

"There's something else," I said. "She said, 'All of us have done some fool things when we were young.' Those were her words. I just want to know what she meant."

"If she went that far, I may as well tell you the rest," Aunt Mel said. "I would have thought she'd be glad enough to keep it to herself instead of starting another round of rumors. To put it plain, she got married the first time when she was fifteen."

I stopped and stared at her. "The first time?"

"She ran off with a boy not much older than she was from across the swamp—one of those families in the Thicket that never come to town except to buy flour and shotgun shells. How they saw enough of each other to know they wanted to marry is beyond me. Anyhow, they went into Beaumont to get a license."

"And?" I had to run to catch up with her and adjust my stride to hers again.

"Well, his folks and Ila's folks caught up with them and brought them home, and that was the end of that."

"But what about the boy?"

"I've got no idea," she said. "I never try to keep track of what those people in the towns inside the Thicket are up to. For all I know, he married someone else and has ten children. Wasn't long after she was sixteen Ila got legally married all right and proper to Evert Hughes."

We walked a little farther, and I said, "Aunt Mel, could I talk to you about Sara?"

This time she was the one who stopped to look at me. We stood there under a tallow tree that had dropped its berries in sticky purple lumps on the sidewalk. Something near the top of the tree was making a rustling sound—probably a bird after the berries. A drop of perspiration tickled as it rolled down my backbone. I waited impatiently for her to answer.

Finally, she said, "Lauren, I gave this matter lots of thought and lots of prayer this morning. I think we should wait until later to get into the subject again. Mrs. Martin is coming this afternoon, and it will be trying enough to go over the story with her. Since Sunday is supposed to be the

Lord's day and a time of rest, let's keep it like that for as much as we can."

"But I think I'd feel better if I could talk to you."

"We all move inside ourselves too much. Dumping emotions on anyone who'll listen doesn't help that much. Forget your feelings about Sara for today, and think about others and what you can do for them. Talk to me tomorrow morning before you go to school."

I hadn't thought about school. Now that the image was in my mind, I dreaded it. We'd all be there—all of us who were at the séance—and I was sure the others wanted to be with me about as much as I wanted to be with them. We would look at each other, and I knew we'd see Sara.

I helped Aunt Mel give the house a final once-over, although it was already spotless and didn't need it. Saturday we had changed sheets on the bed in the extra room, polished all the furniture, swept and vacuumed, and accomplished all the things that make a place look ready for a guest. Aunt Mel had even baked a ham with spices and pineapple rings and had it tucked away in the refrigerator with a big bowl of potato salad. On the side counter in the kitchen, under a clear-plastic cake cover, sat a freshly baked apple cake.

"Even though folks have grief, they still have to eat," Aunt Mel said. "And Monday afternoon will be the funeral."

I shivered when I thought of it. Sara's mother

hadn't wanted her in Houston alive. She didn't want her buried there either. Up here, in the small cemetery at the edge of our piney woods, Sara would lie. And maybe after the funeral no one would ever visit her grave, not even the one who had put her there.

It was after suppertime when Sara's mother arrived, brought to the house by Sheriff Norvell. She was an older, tired image of Sara, like a photograph that is slightly blurred. I knew Aunt Mel wouldn't approve of the woman's tight clothes, the too-short skirt, but she'd never let on, out of common courtesy.

But when the first thing Doris Martin did after introductions was drop into the nearest living-room chair and say, "God, I could use a drink!" Aunt Mel's lips tightened.

Then she answered, "God has seen fit to make this a dry county."

Mrs. Martin cocked her head on one side and looked up at Aunt Mel the way a hen does when she sees someone coming and is trying to figure out if she's going to be fed or caught for the dinner pot.

"You're kidding," she said. "I thought the whole state voted wet a few years ago."

"How long has it been since you lived in these parts?" Aunt Mel said. She was in command of the situation, and in her house no one drank spirits. She sat on the sofa, her long, gaunt frame arranged in the right shape for respectability.

"Not since my husband got killed on that rig accident over near the Louisiana border—about five years ago. Remember?" She looked at us as though reminding us of that accident were the most important thing she could think of.

"Of course," Aunt Mel said sympathetically. "I'm sorry."

It was as though the kindness in her voice had released a floodgate. Mrs. Martin began talking rapidly, her fingers making little tattoos on the arm of the chair. "Everything began to go to pieces after that," she said. "I tried to do for Sara the best I could, but she missed her father, and she carried on something awful when I'd . . . well . . . when I'd date."

She tilted her head and looked at us from the corners of her eyes. "It isn't easy, being without a man, and I'm a woman who needs a man in my life. I—" She stopped, not seeing the responsiveness she had hoped for in our eyes. This time it was Sheriff Norvell who took pity on her. He changed the subject.

"Have any trouble with traffic on your way up here?" he asked.

"No," she said. "That's one thing that hasn't changed. Aside from the local people and folks taking a sidetrack on their way to Louisiana, there aren't too many people interested in coming to this piece of country."

"Oh, I don't know," he said. "We get the travelin' salespeople and the ones who like to come to see the Thicket in the fall and the hunters from the city. Did you hear that Lem Childress claims he saw a panther way back in the Thicket when he was huntin' boar?"

Aunt Mel rose to the occasion with her argument that the panthers had been killed off back in her father's generation and Lem was seeing the result of too much raw liquor, and the conversation was on.

In a little while I excused myself, although nobody really heard me because they were talking about a restaurant the three of them knew about that used to be a hangout over in White Oak until somebody bought that corner, tore the building down, and put in a veterinarian's office and pet hospital.

I went out and sat on the back step. It was dark now, and I couldn't see much because clouds were over the moon. The air was heavy and still and carried the sound of a cricket twanging its back legs in a mating call that went on incessantly. I needed to be by myself. I didn't know what to do.

The back screen door suddenly creaked open, nudging my back, and I jumped. I had startled Mrs. Martin, who was standing there staring at me, her mouth an "O".

"It's all right," I said. "Do you want to come outside?"

She put her feet down carefully on each of the wooden porch steps until she was able to perch beside me. She tucked her skirt around her legs, which didn't accomplish much, pulled a cigarette from a pack, and lit it. Then she turned to me and said, "You aren't going to object to my smoking, too, are you?"

"No," I said. "Did Aunt Mel ask you to smoke outside the house?"

"She's a very prissy lady." The words blew out with a lungful of smoke.

"She's a good-hearted person," I answered. "She's taken care of me since I was little."

"Well, yeah," she said. She looked at me, squinting through the smoke. "I don't understand all this they've told me about Sara. Could you answer some questions for me?"

"I don't think I'll know the answers."

"If you don't, who would?" she countered, and I stopped breathing for an instant.

"Why do you say that? Why me?"

"Don't get huffy. It's just that Sara was staying here. They told me she didn't make friends with the other girls, and sometimes a girl has to talk to another girl, so . . . adding it all up, it comes out you."

"Sara and I . . ." I didn't know quite how to put it. "That is, we weren't the best of friends, and—"

"I understand," she said. "I didn't expect you to be buddies. Sara was a beautiful girl—I have to give her that much—and plain girls are usually jealous of beautiful girls. It's just normal. But since you went to that séance together, I figure she must have told you something about what she had in mind."

I didn't have time to nurse the hurt she had given me. "Does it make any difference now that she's dead?" I asked.

Mrs. Martin let out a long sigh and flicked the butt of her cigarette out into the grass, where it glowed until it winked itself out. "Sheriff Norvell said he thinks Sara might have been murdered. He can't see any other reason for her being in the swamp that way."

She spoke so matter-of-factly about her daughter that I couldn't believe it. I had imagined Mrs. Martin sobbing and fragile, while we all tried to put her together again. That had been bad enough to visualize, but this was worse.

I spoke out suddenly. "When Sara was little, did you hold her on your lap and sing to her and read her stories?"

"Why, yes," she said, not showing any surprise at my question. "When she was little and we had some time in the evenings, when her father was making good money, and I didn't have to work." The words faded like the song at the end of an old record, and I waited in the silence.

"It couldn't last," she finally said. "Nothing good lasts forever."

"But you still loved Sara."

"Of course, I loved her, but Sara was a difficult kid, and she kept running away and telling fibs and hating me for wanting another man, and

79

it just got too much to take. But I loved her. After all, she was my kid."

"But you haven't cried." I was sorry immediately that I had asked, and I gestured toward her, as though I could wipe out the words.

She turned and gave me a long look. "Crying is a luxury," she said, "and I take my luxuries in private, by myself. There are two ways of crying—on the outside and on the inside—and I've been crying on the inside most of my life."

"I'm sorry," I whispered.

"I don't go for all this scary, disappearing stuff," she said. "I know good and well that Sara wouldn't run away alone. Tell me who she went out to meet."

"I can't."

"You can't or you won't?"

She didn't wait for an answer but suddenly got up from the steps, her heels clip-clapping on the boards, and slapped the screen door shut behind her.

It seemed quieter now than it had before Mrs. Martin had come outside. The cricket had stopped, as crickets suddenly do, perhaps because two cricket bodies had come into contact with each other . . . or because something had disturbed the peace of its little spot of night.

It was very quiet.

Over near the hedge I thought I heard a movement, and I got to my feet. It was too dark for shadows, and straining to see into the void, my eyes could detect only rings and rings of black on black, unreal shapes. Something moved.

"Who's out there?" I demanded, my voice too loud.

One of the shapes disentangled itself from the blacker shapes and moved toward me. "It's just me—Fant," he said.

I stayed on my feet. My voice was strained and tight. "Did you want to see Aunt Mel?"

"No, I wanted to see you," he said. He stood at the bottom of the porch steps and looked up at me.

"What about?" I tried not to sound as wary as I felt.

"I just wanted to tell you that I—that Feenie and I—are sorry about all that happened to y'all. I know you girls were squirming in church this morning, but things like that will pass, even though they're hard to take at the time."

He waited, but I didn't know what to say, so he sat on the bottom step, his back to me, and went on. I sat down, too.

"It's hard to believe that anything so horrible could have happened to Sara. She used to like to come over and talk to Feenie, you know."

He craned his neck to look at me, and his eyes were globules that barely shone in the dark. "You must have seen her coming over once in a while to talk to Feenie?"

"Yes," I said. "I remember that." What else could I say?

He turned back, and his shoulders seemed to relax. "I heard that the sheriff thinks Sara left the séance to meet some man to run away with him and thought that disappearing in that strange way would cover her tracks for a while."

"I guess he does think that."

"But the man killed her instead." There was a pause, and he added, "I don't know what kind of sick person would do a thing like that to a pretty girl like Sara. Did she ever talk to y'all about any of the men she—" He stopped and laughed nervously. "I should say 'boys,' not 'men,' at Sara's age, shouldn't I?"

He was uncomfortable again, but not nearly as uncomfortable as I was. I just wanted to get rid of him and get into the house. I had an idea he had been listening to my conversation with Sara's mother, and I didn't know why he was continuing to question me.

I got to my feet, and as I did, he jumped up, facing me.

"I don't know anything about who Sara was meeting, Mr. Lester. She didn't confide in me because we just didn't get along well. That's all there is to it. If I knew anything about who the man—or boy—was, I'd tell Sheriff Norvell. I'd tell everybody right away, so there wouldn't be any guessing about it."

He nodded. We understood each other.

"Good night," I said.

"Good night, Lauren," he answered, and the

dark shape of his body dissolved into the other black shapes in the night. I stood there until I heard the back door of his house open and shut.

I opened our screen door, shut it, and locked it firmly. My fingers were wet, and they trembled against the latch.

7

I overslept the next morning, so I didn't get a chance to talk to Aunt Mel before school. I just bolted down my cereal and toast, scooped up my books, and shouted, "Good-bye!"

"Take this note," Aunt Mel said, hurrying after me to press it into my hand. "It's to get you out of class to attend the funeral."

For a minute I was blank. Then a chill shivered its way up my backbone and around my neck. "But, Aunt Mel—" I began.

She looked at me firmly. "The funeral is this afternoon at two. You be there. Sara has to have someone represent her, and in a way we count as family."

"Her mother will be there."

"Your going will do her mother some good,

too," she said. "No matter what the woman seems like to you, there's still a lot of hurting going on inside her. Having folks with her at the funeral will help her a lot." She threw a quick glance over her shoulder, reassuring herself that Sara's mother was still upstairs and out of hearing range.

"Okay," I said. "I'll come home at one."

As soon as I got to school, I went to the attendance office, handed my note to Miss Plaidy, and watched her eyes and mouth make little movements before the questions came.

"Is it true that Sara Martin was murdered?" she asked, leaning as far toward me over the counter as her puffed-up pigeon-breasted body would permit her to lean.

"I don't know," I said.

"I heard she was running away, hitchhiking down the highway into Houston."

"I don't know."

"Somebody said she heard there was a tramp involved. You hear anything about that?"

I backed away from the counter. "Could I have my permit to leave class, please?"

She looked at me with the antagonism she'd show if I were accused of stealing a first grader's milk money, scribbled something on a pink slip of paper, and thrust it at me.

"Thanks," I said automatically, and raced outside to gulp huge breaths of the clear, warm air. I could smell the perfume of loblolly pines mingling with sweet bay, muscadine, and the wet cypress trees that rise from the swamp water in the Thicket. "Oh, dear God!" I said, remembering the dense darkness of the Thicket and Sara Martin lying drowned in the swamp. I sat down on the nearest step.

A couple of the kids going past me, up and down the stairs, paused and looked at me, decided I was all right, and kept going. But Carley Hughes sat down next to me.

"Are you okay?" he asked.

I nodded.

"You look kind of strange. You aren't going to faint or anything like that?"

"No," I said. "I'm all right. I just had a session with that old you-know-what in the attendance office, and it made me mad, and I thought about Sara, and—I don't know—it was all too much for me at once, I guess."

He didn't answer, so I added, "I'm getting out of class to go to her funeral."

"I'm glad you're going." His voice was low. I noticed that he had a death grip on his notebook, and the knuckles on the backs of his hands stood out like the ridges in a freshly plowed field. "Somebody besides her mother should be there," he added. "I think some of her friends should be there."

"Are you going?"

"Yes," he said, and he looked out over the lawn and trees.

"You were one of Sara's friends."

Carley turned and gave me an appraising look. "What are you trying to tell me, Lauren?"

"I'm not trying to tell you anything. I only said that you were Sara's friend."

"You lived in the same house with Sara. She talked to you, didn't she?"

"Of course she talked to me. We weren't mad at each other."

"I mean, well . . . talked about what she was doing, anybody she liked . . . that sort of thing."

I took a deep breath and stared at Carley. "Why are you going all around the bush? Why don't you just come right out and ask me if I know who Sara was going to meet that night?"

"You know that she was going to meet someone?" One of his eyebrows raised a little, punctuating his question.

I was confused, off guard, and I stammered like a child. "Why . . . why should you question me? How am I supposed to know Sara's secrets? Sara didn't confide in me!"

"Don't come undone," he said, and he turned his gaze away. "I didn't mean to get you upset. I didn't want to grill you with questions. I just . . . well, I really care that Sara died. Do you understand that?"

There were tears in the corners of his eyes, and I impulsively reached over and put a hand on his arm. "I understand."

I thought how crazy Sara had been for going off

with whoever had killed her instead of sticking around and falling in love with Carley. He would have married her someday and done his best to make her happy. He was that kind of person, I knew.

Carley stood up abruptly, said, "See you," and disappeared in the group of people who were coming up the stairs. I stood up, too, and went to my first-period class. Roberta wasn't in school, and I wished I could have cut out the way she had.

I'm not sure what went on that morning. My mind wasn't on my work. Come to think of it, no one seemed to be with it. Everyone had a half-distracted look. Word had got around that Sheriff Norvell suspected that Sara had been murdered, and we were all uncomfortable with the idea. The crime of murder was one that belonged in the city or on television, not in our little town, not up here in East Texas, where everyone knew everyone and murder didn't fit.

Maddie grabbed my arm as I entered the cafeteria at lunchtime. "We've all got to talk," she said.

"Here?" It was all I could think of to say.

"Why not? This is where we planned it all, isn't it?"

I nodded. I saw Allie coming. She hesitated as though she wished she could run in the other direction. Then she took a deep breath and joined us.

"I suppose we all have to talk about this sooner

or later," I said, "but here in the cafeteria we're likely to be interrupted."

"Yeah?" One of Maddie's eyebrows curved up as the corners of her mouth went in the opposite direction. "You haven't noticed that people have been avoiding us?"

I hadn't. I'd been too full of myself to notice anything.

Allie was next to me now, peeping out through windows of self-protection. "We'll meet at the corner table," Maddie told her.

Allie and I had brought sack lunches, so we went directly to the table. Luemma was already there, chewing on her fingernails. In a few minutes Dana trailed along behind Maddie, and we all slung our legs over the benches, feeling insulated from the others in the cafeteria but not really wanting to be together again.

"Where's Roberta?" I asked.

"Absent today," Maddie said.

"She's lucky," Luemma muttered. She turned to Maddie. "Just like you were lucky yesterday to miss that hellfire sermon."

"It wasn't luck," Maddie said.

"You mean you just pretended to have cramps?"

"Keep it down," Maddie growled at her. "This isn't the sex-ed class."

"It doesn't matter," I said.

"Yes, it does," Luemma said. She pulled a strand of hair away from her mouth and pouted. "That means Maddie was cheating."

89

"And one of us is cheating about the séance," Allie whispered, her eyes staring at a point above our heads. "Someone locked that door behind Sara when she left. Someone knew she was going to leave."

There was a long period of silence. Then Luemma said, "Roberta isn't here."

"We can't accuse her just because she isn't here," I said. "I think we should have this meeting some other time." I looked at my watch. "I'm going to leave in the middle of my next class. Aunt Mel wants me home so I can go to the funeral."

"I'm going to the funeral, too," Allie said.

"We all are, aren't we?" Maddie asked.

Everyone nodded.

"I didn't even like her," Maddie said.

In the void that followed, Allie's strained voice came out as chipper as a young sparrow's when the sun comes up. "My goodness! It's almost time for the bell, and isn't it funny? None of us have even opened our lunches!"

Maddie mumbled something vulgar, got up, and stalked out of the cafeteria. Dana and Luemma left without a word. Allie turned to me and there were tears in her eyes.

"Lauren," she said, "I thought about something, and the idea scares me."

When I didn't answer, she gripped my arm, and I could feel the dampness of her fingers, the electric urgency that trembled through them to my arm. "Lauren, what if one of us was . . . well—"

She stopped, and I said, "What are you trying to ask me, Allie?"

"About the séance," she stammered. "I mean, what if the person who locked the door behind Sara was working with the murderer?"

I gasped, and she leaned toward me, her face as pale as new cream. "What if one of us helped murder Sara?"

My voice was shaking as much as my hands as I said, "Don't even think a thing like that, Allie! It couldn't be possible! Just forget about it!"

She nodded and tried a quavering smile. I managed to pick up my books, throw my unopened lunch sack into the trash can, and head for my next class. What Allie had said shook me more than I could ever let her know.

There are some days in which every minute is a pain to be wrenched through, and that day was one of them. When I finally made it home, I washed my face, brushed my hair, and went downstairs to get something to eat.

The house looked extra-clean, to the point of being unreal. The sideboard in the dining room sagged under platters of casseroles and salads and cakes. Even though Sara hadn't been one of us, Aunt Mel was a fixture in town, and all the neighbor ladies came through in style, making sure, as they always did, that when people gathered in a house after the funeral, there would be plenty to eat and the grieving women of the house wouldn't have to go to the trouble of cooking for a crowd.

Aunt Mel handed me a tall glass of iced tea. "Take this outside and sit with Mrs. Martin. She's on the back steps, smoking again, and she needs someone to talk to."

I took it and obediently went out to the back porch, where I sat on the top step, nodding to Mrs. Martin and sipping from the glass as an excuse not to speak. There were mascara smudges under her eyes and colorless places on her cheeks where she had rubbed the tears and the foundation makeup away.

"This is the hardest thing I've ever had to do in my whole life," she said to me.

I nodded. I tried to think of the right words to say, but they wouldn't come. I was still trying to get rid of the shock of Allie's suspicions.

In a few minutes she said, "I don't know why I came. Who makes the rules that say someone has to come to someone else's funeral? What good does it do anyone?"

"You're Sara's mother," I said.

"Mother," she repeated slowly, as though tasting the word. "There are mothers, and there are mothers. Some mothers get greeting cards on Mother's Day, and go to PTA meetings, and bake cookies, and . . . go to funerals. Those are mothers. But then there are people like me. It's been a long time since I've really thought of myself as Sara's mother, and even then, I don't think I was ever a good mother."

"Maybe if your husband hadn't died, things would have been better for you and Sara," I said.

She laughed humorlessly. "Don't bet on it. Our marriage didn't have far to go."

"I'm sorry." I didn't know what else to say.

With the heel of one shoe she ground out her cigarette butt viciously, pulverizing it into the wooden step. "I'd better get ready to go," she said. "It's almost time."

I didn't have any sympathy for Mrs. Martin, either then or at the funeral. All I wanted to do was close my eyes, hold my breath, and wake up to find it was over and done with.

Since Aunt Mel and I had to sit in the front pew of the church with Mrs. Martin, I didn't pay attention to who was at the service. But at the graveyard, which is on a little rise of a hill west of town, I looked around at the ring of mourners and felt even worse. Under the heat of the afternoon sun, which beat against the leaves of the ancient dusty oaks, each of us from the séance stood alone. Like so many pillars of salt, we had tried to look back and failed. And in the eyes of the others who shared the pale, flat sky with us, there was sometimes suspicion, sometimes a little fear.

Carley Hughes was there as he had promised. He didn't look at the coffin but stared off across the hill to the roofs of the town and the dark pines of the Big Thicket beyond. Sheriff Norvell's glance darted from one face to another with the persistence of a pesky bottlefly. Once, when his eyes met mine, I stared right back at him until my eyes watered, and I had to look down, blinking back the sting of the tears.

I moved with Aunt Mel and Mrs. Martin to the grave site as the coffin with Sara Martin's body in it was lowered into the pit. The reddish earth had a damp, cold smell, and I shivered, even though the heat of the sun was sticky against my back.

Our minister did pretty well, I thought. He mostly recited verses from the bible instead of saying nice, personal things about Sara. He really didn't know Sara. None of us had.

Finally it was over. I knew Mrs. Martin was going to stop by the house only long enough to collect her things. Then she'd leave for Houston. I didn't want to go back to the chicken salad and chocolate cake and waggling tongues and prying eyes.

"I'm going to take a walk, Aunt Mel," I whispered, and she nodded her permission.

I watched Mrs. Martin drift to Aunt Mel's car in the center of a patting, murmuring huddle of comfort. I could feel her loneliness, and for the first time I understood the chill of loneliness Sara must have felt. I knew what it was like to be lonely.

Like the last drops of water in an overturned glass, everyone soon disappeared, and there was no one at the grave site but me and the caretaker, who had folded up the chairs into a neat pile on a cart and was already filling the grave.

"Oh, Sara. Poor, lonely Sara. Who did you go to meet?" My mind reached out, and the answer came back: "Find out."

"I owe you that much," I said aloud.

The caretaker raised his head to stare at me, and I turned and ran toward the entrance gate, toward the road into town.

As I walked, I sorted out my thoughts. I didn't know how I was going to find out who Sara had met if Sheriff Norvell couldn't. I had no idea, no clue. I didn't know where to begin. I had to talk to someone. Not Aunt Mel. She wouldn't have time, with feeding the people who would have come to the house and getting Mrs. Martin on her way back to Houston. Maybe I could talk to Allie.

I sighed. No, I couldn't. Allie would just be upset and frightened. I couldn't talk to any of the girls I knew.

I was coming down Oak Lane when it struck me. Of course! I could talk to Ila Hughes. She'd be between shifts at the café and at home, most probably. She had invited me to come and see her. Besides, I was intrigued by Carley's grandmother. She was a strange woman, wiry and young for a grandmother but filled with all the old tales and superstitions of an even older generation. She had a way of getting her face close to the people she was talking to and peering at them over the top of her glasses.

Now I knew she had a past, a past that colored in the edges and made her more interesting. Yes. I would go to the Hughes house and see if Mrs. Hughes had time to talk to me. I would tell her everything I knew about Sara. Maybe then I would know what to do and where to start.

I walked up the driveway to her house, squeezing carefully between the dented old car and a prickly hedge. I could see Mrs. Hughes through the open kitchen door. Over the doorway was the traditional horseshoe, upturned to catch good luck. The screen door was held to with a hook, and she was seated at a green painted kitchen table, stringing beans. I knocked on the edge of the screen door, making it rattle.

She looked up quickly, recognized me, and smiled. Putting down the pan of beans, she got up and opened the door. "Come in, Lauren," she said. "I'm trying to take care of Carley's supper for tonight."

I followed her in, and she went back to the beans. I wandered around the large kitchen, looking at all the clutter that comes from years of collecting things. "I never thought about you having to come home and make supper and then go back to the café to serve meals to other people," I said. "Wouldn't it be easier for both of y'all to eat supper over there?"

"It wouldn't work out for Carley," she said. "They serve too many starches at the café. Carley needs balanced meals."

I could see the pride she had in Carley. It was as good a way to get into our conversation as any.

"Has Carley had any offers of scholarships yet?" I asked.

She straightened and glowed as though her batteries had been switched to "on." "The whole thing is a wonderment," she answered. "The high school coach says Texas, Texas Tech, and A & M have been asking after Carley. He says Carley won't have any trouble getting a good scholarship. The boy's only problem will be in making up his mind where to go."

"That's great," I said.

"If I only knew things like that could happen, his daddy might have gone on to higher schooling, too," she said. "If he'd had more education, he could have had an easier life, and he wouldn't have been in a low-paying job at the lumber mill when Darla went to pick him up and . . ." She shook her head briskly. "There are good things ahead for Carley. Maybe he'll be an engineer, maybe a doctor."

I had never known Carley to show much interest in anything except baseball. What she said surprised me.

"If he went into medicine," I said, "maybe he could come back here and take old Dr. Lewis's place. Dr. Lewis will be ready to retire soon."

"No," she said, and her fingers paused on the beans. "He'll stay in the city—Houston or Dallas most likely—and make good money. I don't want him to come back here."

"But won't you miss him?"

97

She shrugged. "I'll see him once in a while. The city isn't too far away."

If Ila Hughes had been able to run away with the boy she was marrying, would they have gone on to a city to stay, or would they have been drawn back home again? I wondered if everything she had wanted for herself she now wanted for Carley. She didn't have much now: a kitchen that smelled of herbs, spices, and strange woodsy odors; a full-time job; and a grandson.

I had made my way past the kitchen windowsill with its bunches of dried leaves and odd-sized bottles and jars containing slips of plants growing in them, the roots stringing out through the water in tiny white fingers. I was standing before the stone fireplace in the corner, thinking how unusual it was to have a fireplace in a kitchen, when my glance fell on something that made me automatically step back. On the mantel, on a level with my eyes, was a row of little gray skulls!

There was a chuckle close to my ear, and Mrs. Hughes touched my shoulders, moving me forward again. "Those are my little birds," she said, laughing. "Aren't they precious? Little bird skulls. I began finding them in the Thicket years ago."

She picked up one and held it out to me. "Here, take it. Hold it. Feel how smooth it is. Look at the tiny beak."

I held it in my fingers gingerly. It seemed so vulnerable, so weird with the wide hole where the neck had been, and the gaping sockets for the tiny eyes. The beak curved over my index finger, and its point was sharp.

She took it from me and placed it back with care on the mantel, where it joined the others, mock guardians of the room.

Mrs. Hughes began to laugh again. "It's really a joke," she said. "All the birds, and the cat can't get to them."

I looked around the room. "You have a cat?"

"Don't you know where?" She winked at me. "In the fireplace."

I didn't say anything. I just walked around to the other side of the table, so that Ila Hughes wouldn't be between me and the door.

For a moment she looked puzzled. Then she shook her head, grinned, and said, "For goodness' sakes, Lauren. Is this the first house you've been in where a cat was buried somewhere inside the walls to keep the devil away? I thought everybody knew about that."

"I've never heard about that," I mumbled.

She bustled over to the table, pulled out a chair, and motioned me toward it. Automatically I sat down.

"Well, my father went by the tradition of his family," she said. "They all came from England, and apparently had been doing that for years over there—burying a cat in the walls. Over there they had those thick walls, you know. Here my father had to use the stones of the fireplace."

"Your house must be very old," I said. It sounded stupid, but at least I could talk again. I wondered if Aunt Mel knew about the cat in the Hughes fireplace.

Mrs. Hughes folded her hands neatly on the table and rested her weight on her elbows. "I'm glad you came by," she said. "I don't have time for friends during the day, and I like to talk to people."

"It was nice of you to invite me to come," I said politely. "I guess . . . well, I wanted to talk, too. I thought maybe I could talk to you." The little bird skulls stared down at me, and I wondered now if I really wanted to.

"You want to talk about what went on at that séance?"

"Partly."

"Whose idea was it to have the séance?" she asked. She got up, ran some water over the beans, and put them on the back of the stove. She wiped her hands down the sides of her apron and sat down at the table again. "You want some iced tea?" she asked.

"No, thanks," I said. "I really don't want anything right now." It took me a moment to remember her question, and I frowned. "I really can't think of how the séance idea got started. Roberta was talking a lot about her psychic powers and all that, and Sara said it would be fun to have a séance, and then . . . well, the next thing I remember was that Roberta set the time and place because her parents were going to be out of town, and we just went. That's all."

"What was the reason for the séance then? Just fun?"

"Fun," I echoed bitterly. "I didn't really want to go."

"Why did you?"

"Because Sara wanted me to go."

Mrs. Hughes rested her arms on the table, peered over the top of her glasses, and said, "There was something very wrong about that séance. When y'all called up those spirits, you didn't know what evil forces you were playing games with. The bad spirits work on the dark side of men. They got that girl out of the house with the doors locked."

There were prickles along my backbone. I wished her face weren't so close to mine. Her eyes seemed watery and transparent, giving me the feeling that if I looked hard enough, I could see through them into her skull. I shivered.

"Sheriff Norvell thinks someone opened the door for Sara, then locked it again." I wondered why I was whispering.

"Sheriff Norvell is guessing," she said. "There are things that he'll never know about, because he tries to find all his facts in this world. If someone let Sara out and locked the door, it would be planned, and that person would know who Sara was going to meet, and she'd tell the sheriff, and there wouldn't be any guessing. He'd know how Sara died, wouldn't he?"

"But—"

"You see. I'm right, and the sheriff is wrong. That Roberta—tell me about her. Tell me all about what she did and what happened at the séance." Mrs. Hughes's eyes glistened wetly with her eagerness to hear.

I was so disappointed that for a few moments I couldn't speak. I had hoped that Mrs. Hughes would let me talk and would listen and, when I had finished, would nod her head wisely and advise me about what to do next. But she was acting more like Miss Plaidy in the attendance office. She just wanted to find out the inside story, probably so she could tell her customers at the café.

Before I could say anything, the front door opened and closed with a bang, and Carley loped through the house and into the kitchen. He stopped short when he saw me, and there was a question in his eyes as he looked at his grandmother.

"I didn't know anyone was here," he said. "Did you come to see me, Lauren?"

I pushed back my chair and got to my feet. "I was walking close by and just stopped in to talk with your grandmother," I said.

"Oh. Well, you want to stick around?"

"No," I said. "I've got to get home and start on my history assignment."

102

He turned to Mrs. Hughes. "Could I have supper an hour early? We're having night practice."

"All right," she said. Then she turned to me. "We didn't have much time to talk."

"That's okay," I said. "There wasn't anything really important to talk about."

All the way home I scuffed through the early-fall leaves that had begun to drop, crumpled bits of gold and red and brown. There was no point in asking anyone else what I should do. I was bewildered by Mrs. Hughes's reaction, but it showed me that I would have to make my decisions by myself.

I sighed as I wondered. Was there anyone I could trust?

8

People who don't have much to occupy their minds talk a lot, and the men who sit for hours in front of Snyder's drugstore with nothing to do but spin yarns built the story of Sara's death into a full-length feature over the next two days.

Some began to complain that the sheriff wasn't doing his job, that the murderer should be caught forthwith. Some stared slantwise at any of us who had been at the séance and talked about people's knowing things and not telling and how they should be made to tell.

Others wouldn't let go of the preternatural aspects of the séance, especially after one of them recalled the true happenings of Effie Bruger's youngest brother. He had kept talking about a ghost in the old barn that used to stand on the same property the Campions were renting. Somehow the barn caught fire while the Bruger boy and his friends were ghost hunting, and he got a bad burn on his left arm. The scars were still on it, they said, when he grew up and left for work in the Oklahoma oilfields. They were in a strange pattern, like rays from a sun.

Mrs. Granbery fingered the stone amulet she wore around her neck and remembered that just five years ago old Blinky Parrs saw something in the Thicket that gave him fits, and after that he never was quite right in the head.

Ila Hughes told her customers that she had heard an owl hoot twice that very night and knew that something bad would come of it. "You don't fool around with evil spirits," she added.

And I guess I clung to a kind of crazy hope that it hadn't happened, that Sara had never come to stay with us, that all the memories would drift off like winter fogs. Then Sheriff Norvell phoned and said he was getting all the girls together who were at that first séance, to recreate what had been said and done.

"Another séance?" My voice shook.

"Near as what happened last time as y'all can make it," he said.

"Do we have to?"

"Yes," he said. "I figure it will help me get things into their proper places. There's a lot more I need to know about this whole thing."

"I really don't want . . ." I began.

105

"Y'got a pencil? Then write down the time and place," he said without giving me a chance to answer.

So I did. It was Roberta's house again, that evening. I put down the phone and told Aunt Mel.

"Would you like to go with me?" I asked her.

Aunt Mel had stopped for a cup of tea, and her fingers were moving so quickly over her knitting wool that it looked like a form of incantation. She looked at me inquisitively.

"If Ashe wants to re-create the séance, then he doesn't want a passel of others around, too."

"I have to go alone?"

"You went before."

"But not alone." I hunched down on her hassock, pulled my knees close to my chest and looked up at her. There were tears in my eyes, and I was trying to keep them from spilling over. "I'm scared, Aunt Mel."

She studied me, and I could see a softness in her face that I had never noticed there before. The thought came to me that maybe I had seen it often but hadn't paid attention. It was like seeing my Aunt Melvamay for the first time, the way it is when your best friend gives you her senior picture. You take a long, hard look and suddenly see that she is a different person from the one you thought you'd been looking at all through school. It gives you a strange feeling that something happened while you weren't watching.

"If you like, I'll walk with you," she said. "No

sense in taking the car for that short a distance."

I sighed with relief. "Then you'll come inside with me?"

"No," she said. "I'll just wait outside until you're ready to leave and walk home with you."

Now the tears spilled over, and I leaned against her legs, wrapping my arms around them. "I need you, Aunt Mel," I said.

"I'm here," she answered, and the clack of her knitting needles stopped briefly as she rested her hand on my head. It was as good as a blessing.

"I didn't know anything was going to happen to Sara," I said.

"Of course you didn't," she answered, the clicking of her needles punctuating her words. "What time should you be there?"

"At seven."

"Then we'll have supper a bit early. The beef should be tender soon. Suppose you set the table and scrape some carrots for me. Cut them in good-sized chunks, and put them in with the beef."

I rubbed away the moisture from my cheeks with the back of my hand. "Okay," I said. Things had settled back to normal on the surface. I could put tonight into the back compartment of my mind. Scraping the fat orange carrots didn't mix with preternatural fears.

By seven, as we headed down the road, the moon was already high. It looked slimmed down, like a fat lady on a crash diet, still full, but not quite bursting at the seams. The light it shed was paler, too, and I stumbled twice over holes in the dirt road.

"Slow down," Aunt Mel said, putting a firm hand on my arm. "No sense in racing toward trouble."

"You think there's going to be trouble? What kind of trouble?"

"The only thing I know for sure in this life is that I can't be sure about anything. What I said was just an expression."

"It seemed more real than just an expression."

"That's because you're disturbed, Lauren."

I thought I felt someone behind us, and I turned quickly, stumbling again, righting myself through Aunt Mel's steady arm.

"What are you afraid of?" she asked.

"I wish I knew. I'm afraid of whoever killed Sara."

"No one has proof it was murder."

"But there isn't anything logical about Sara's being in the Thicket, for any reason."

"It's never logical when a young person runs away. The only reason they're running away is that they're being illogical."

"Someone we know could have killed her."

"If she were murdered, it could have been a stranger, a man who picked her up if she were hitchhiking."

"It could be someone we know," I repeated.

"Let the sheriff worry about that," Aunt Mel said.

"What if this person decided to kill somebody else?"

"Who, for instance?"

"Someone who might know who he is."

"Do you know who he is, Lauren?" She stopped in the road, staring at me.

"Of course I don't!" I was almost shouting. "If I did, I would have told you, or the sheriff, or someone—everyone! But the murderer doesn't know that! He might think I know and I'm just afraid to tell anyone yet and might talk about it later!"

She nodded. "I thought about that," she said.

It cleared my head, and I stopped ranting. "You did?"

"I've always taken care of you. I'm not going to stop now."

I began to laugh. "But, Aunt Mel! What could you do if a killer were after me?"

She opened her purse, and there in the moonlight shone the metal from the gun her father used to keep on top of the bookcase, hidden from sight. She had shown it to me once when she was up there, dusting. I was sure it had never been fired—at least not by her.

"Oh, Aunt Mel, I love you!" I said, and I hugged her. She patted me awkwardly. She wasn't used to demonstrations of affection. But that gun in her purse and her presence on this lonely road meant more to me than anything else she could have said or done.

"We'll be late," she said quietly, and without another word we went up the road until we got to the Campion house.

The sheriff's car was there, and a couple of others in the front yard. Henry Krump, Allie's father, sat behind the wheel of his pickup truck, the glowing end of his cigarette moving in the darkness.

"Go on inside," Aunt Mel told me. "I'll be perfectly safe waiting out here for you."

I went into the house, knees trembling, after Mrs. Campion opened the door. I found the others sitting like a row of stiff-backed penguins at the zoo, waiting . . . waiting. No one was talking to anyone else. Maddie was scowling, and Luemma's lower lip curled out in a pout.

"Is everyone here?" When nothing came out, I cleared my throat and asked again.

"You're next to last," Sheriff Norvell said. "We're waiting on Roberta."

"Roberta?" I slid onto the sofa next to Allie. "But this is her house. Why isn't she here?"

Her mother, a drab woman who didn't look a bit like Roberta, shrugged nervously and twisted her hands together so hard it seemed as though she'd break her fingers. "Roberta went out around six," she said. "I sent her to the store, as I usually do, because I've got a bad back, and she can carry those big sacks better than I can and . . ."

She went on, and I could tell from Sheriff Norvell's expression that he'd heard the story before. He looked pointedly at his wristwatch, which was half hidden in the folds of skin around his wrist. "Shouldn't take her this long to get back. Was she troubled about goin' through this séance thing again?"

"She's a good girl," her mother stammered. "She's always been interested in dramatic things, mysterious things. But she wouldn't do anything she shouldn't. She wouldn't have hurt that Martin girl."

"Didn't say she would," the sheriff said.

"She wanted to make friends. She . . . it was just for fun, she said. She didn't mean for anyone to get hurt over it."

"Why didn't she want to be here?"

"She wouldn't run off!" Mrs. Campion was getting excited, and her finger twisting was grotesque. It hurt to watch her hands. "She thinks you blame her, that you think she had something to do with it because it was here, at our house. But she wouldn't run off!"

"We'll give her a few more minutes," the sheriff said. He turned to the rest of us, his glance sweeping across and back like a searchlight. "Y'all can help me by taking the same places you were in before."

"I don't remember," Dana said. She looked blank, and her chin quivered.

111

"There. You were sitting over there," Maddie volunteered. She pointed with a trembling finger.

"And I was here," Luemma said, "and Allie was next to Lauren."

We slowly, reluctantly, moved to the floor and sat in the places we had taken before. There was a wide gap where Sara and Roberta had been sitting side by side. It was scary, staring at that gap, knowing both girls had been there. I wished Roberta would hurry and get back.

Someone, probably Roberta, had put the candle and vase of periwinkles on a side table. The sheriff had Dana place them in the center of the circle, just as they had been. He turned off all the lights except for the one lamp.

"Now what?" he asked.

We all looked at each other.

"Suppose one of y'all fills me in on what happened."

"I remember that Allie wanted to know if the doors were locked, because she was scared," Luemma said.

"We were all scared as hell," Maddie added. "I checked the front door, and Allie checked the back door. They were both locked, with a dead bolt on the front door and a chain on the back one."

"That right?" he asked Allie.

She nodded agreement.

"So then what?"

"Then Roberta said we were going to light the

candle and turn off all the lights, I think," Maddie said.

There was a silence, and he finally said, "Go on."

"We can't," I told him. "It has to be Roberta. I don't remember how she did it, but she acted like she was in a trance and said things that were kind of strange, and she got messages from somebody in the room."

"Who?"

"We couldn't see anyone."

"Y'all are telling me you think some . . . thing, some spirit, was here in the room with you?"

"I don't know," I said. "I felt something. That's all."

"I did, too!" Allie said. "I was so scared I felt sick to my stomach!"

There was an instantaneous babble as we all tried to tell him what the mood was like, how frightened we were; and he got five very different versions of what Sara had said and what she had done.

"So one of you show me how she fell on the candle," he said.

None of us moved.

"Come on. You do it, Lauren."

"No," I said.

"Why not?"

"It's . . . it's too final. It's like putting myself in Sara's place. I can't."

113

"I don't think we should do this," Maddie said in a low voice. "I feel something now, right in this room." She seemed to peer into even the dusty corners of the room, as though searching for someone.

"Don't do that, Maddie!" Allie whispered.

Maddie shivered. "Don't you feel it, too?" she asked us, without looking at us, still staring around the room.

"Feel what?" I managed to ask.

"Sara," Maddie said.

Allie gave a little cry, and Maddie added, "This is too damn strong for us. The purpose of a séance is to contact the dead, and I don't want any part of it!"

"We can't go on with this!" I said. I stood up, tugging Allie with me because she was clinging to my arm like moss on the limbs of an oak. Dana jumped up and sat in a chair. Luemma shook her head, her arms wrapped around her shoulders, as she hugged herself.

"Where is Roberta anyway?" Luemma said. "I want to get this over and go home!"

"Where's Roberta? That's a good question," Sheriff Norvell said. "I think it's time I went lookin' for her. The rest of y'all can go home now. Y'all have given me enough for the moment. That is, unless someone wants to speak up and offer more information, something that will tell us how Sara got through a locked door?"

But Roberta's mother was moving in on the

sheriff, saying, "You do think Roberta's all right, don't you? I mean, she wouldn't just not show up unless—"

I couldn't stand it. I hurried outside to join Aunt Mel, who was calmly leaning against the pickup truck, talking to Allie's father. He sighed with relief when he saw us, started his engine, and called, "See you soon, Mel."

"Wasn't too bad, was it?" Aunt Mel asked as we walked toward home.

"Roberta didn't show up," I told her.

"That's odd," she said. "Roberta wouldn't run off, would she?"

"Her mother said she wouldn't, and she said Roberta wasn't involved in any way with Sara's leaving the séance."

"Then what in the world happened to Roberta?"

Two days later Aunt Mel's question was answered when a botanist from the university drove in from the Thicket at a speed high enough to raise a dust cloud that wouldn't settle for an hour. In the trunk of his car, wrapped up in a tarpaulin, was Roberta Campion's body.

9

Anyone who had thought Sara's death was accidental was silenced. There was no doubt now but that Sara—and Roberta—had been murdered, although there were still some who claimed, with lowered voices and slithering eyes, that the devil and his evil ones come for their own and that people who fool around with séances and call on the dead are just asking for what they're going to get.

Late that night the phone rang, and I hurried to answer it, hoping it wouldn't wake Aunt Mel.

"Who is the murderer?" The voice came in a whisper, stretching through the darkness like a cold chill.

"Who are you?"

"Murderer!" the voice accused.

"Tell me who you are! Tell me!" I demanded frantically even though I knew whoever it was had hung up and the line was dead.

Aunt Mel was there in the darkness, her nightgown flapping around her legs. "Who frightened you?" she asked.

I told her about the call, and she made an angry noise in the back of her throat. "Busybodies!"

"Someone wants to hurt me."

"Not whoever made that call," she said. "Just some stupid busybody who had nothing else on his mind." She put an arm around my shaking shoulders. "You get back to bed, and from now on I'll answer all phone calls."

"But, Aunt Mel—"

"It's decided," she said.

There were more calls, but when whoever was phoning found he had only Aunt Mel to reckon with, they stopped. Then there was an obscene printed note in the mail, addressed to me. I couldn't even finish reading it. I just let out a strangled gasp, and Aunt Mel took it out of my hands.

"I'll open the mail, too," she said. If there were any more letters, I didn't know about them. Aunt Mel said anything that came would be turned over to the sheriff.

"Who would do this?" I asked her.

"There are a lot of sick minds in this world," she said. "Some of them are inside people who look very normal on the outside, people you live next to and work with every day in the week. When something fearful happens to disrupt the pattern of their lives, they react."

"But it doesn't make sense."

"Neither do they," she said.

Luemma's mother phoned Aunt Mel. Luemma had received the same phone calls and mail and had gone to bed with nervous indigestion. She wanted to send Luemma to stay with an aunt in Arkansas, but the sheriff wouldn't let the girl leave town. She was so indignant I could hear her voice vibrating from across the room. She wouldn't allow Luemma to leave the house, not even for school.

Allie told me that she and Maddie and Dana had all got the same messages. "Maybe we should have another meeting," she said.

"About what?" I asked. I felt that things were happening so fast that I had missed something I should have paid attention to. But would a meeting of the five of us help? I didn't think so. "We really have nothing to talk about, do we?"

Allie shrugged. "What's going to happen, Lauren?"

"I wish I knew," I said.

Church attendance went way up, and people began remembering all kinds of stories about witch water in the Thicket, and a giant black panther with human eyes, and old Marley Thompson, who cast hex spells on people until he accidentally shot off his right foot while hunting and went to live

118

with his son and daughter-in-law in Buffalo, where it's too cold to pay attention to hex spells.

Feenie came over for a glass of iced tea, and she sat in the chair with its back to the front window. Her cropped dark hair wisped out in little points around her head like a cap, and she wiped away the perspiration on her forehead with the back of one arm.

"What gets me," she said, "is why these two girls were drowned. Who'd have it in for them?"

"It's anybody's guess," Aunt Mel said. She reached for her knitting and began a steady tattoo with the needles.

"Folks say that Sara thought she was going to meet a man she knew and run off with him," Feenie said. "You believe that?"

She was staring straight at me, so I stammered, "I guess so."

"Who was he?"

"I—I have no idea. Sara didn't confide in me."

"Girls always tell each other private things—especially about boys." Even with the sun at Feenie's back, I could see her eyes, and they were narrow, sharp pinpoints of light. Her glance was drilling into me, exploring me. So . . . Feenie had also been aware of Sara's visits next door. What did Feenie know? I wondered. And what did she think I knew?

"Sara and Lauren didn't get along too well. They didn't exchange confidences," Aunt Mel said calmly. "You want some oatmeal cookies, Feenie?

I know you don't like to bake much. Maybe I could wrap up some for you to take home with you. Fant has always liked my cookies."

Feenie was distracted. "Cookies? Oh . . . thanks, Mel, but I haven't been feeling well lately, and I've got to watch my diet. Gallbladder again, I think. You know . . . that pain over here." She stretched and rubbed the spot that was bothering her while Aunt Mel politely clucked over it.

"Ought to see the doctor," Aunt Mel said.

"I suppose. I keep putting it off." Feenie turned to me again, but I met her stare straight on, keeping my mind as blank as possible.

"Whyn't you run over to Allie's house, Lauren?" Aunt Mel asked me. "You've been around the house too much lately. Time to get out and get some fresh air."

Gratefully I mumbled good-byes and left the house. I didn't head for Allie's house. I didn't want to talk to Allie. There was nothing she could help me with. I was always the strong one, and Allie leaned on me the way our three-legged table leans against the steady squat old sofa. If I tried to lean on Allie, I was pretty sure there would be nothing left but emotional disaster and a splintered friendship.

I walked for maybe half an hour, maybe an hour. My blouse was sticking to my back, and my jeans were rough against my damp legs. It was too hot to stay outside, yet I didn't want to go home. I wasn't sure what I wanted. I was tired, I was mixed up, and I was afraid of someone I probably knew, who had a blank face and strong, drowning hands.

I was close to home, in front of the Clooney house, when I realized a car had slowed down behind me and was pulling near the curb, pacing me. I whirled to see Sheriff Norvell steering with one hand and struggling with the window crank, trying to roll the window down. As I stopped to stare at him, he put his foot on the brake, bringing the car to a jerking halt.

He muttered something under his breath as he rolled the window all the way down, then called, "Lauren, get in the car. I want to talk to you."

"Why can't we talk here?"

"I'm not about to lean outa this window, yellin' at you on the street. That's why. Now, come on around to the passenger side, and get in so we can talk."

I looked up and down the street. There was no one in sight. I didn't want to get in the car with the sheriff, but there didn't seem to be a choice. I pushed away all the little nightmares of imagination and dutifully did as he asked.

He struggled with the window again, this time putting it up tightly. The air conditioner blew a steady blast of cool air into my face, cutting a path through the cigar smoke, and it steadied me.

"Had this car two years now," he grunted, his face popping red blotches in his exertion with the window handle. "They never can get this damned

121

window fixed proper." Finally, he leaned back against the seat and said, "I came by your place to talk to you, and I was just cuttin' over to the drugstore when I saw you comin' down the street. Where you been?"

"What difference does it make?"

"Don't get lippy," he said. "You've always been a good kid, kept your nose clean and made your Aunt Mel glad to have you around. Don't get lippy and spoil things."

"I'm sorry," I mumbled.

He pulled away from the curb and turned the corner.

"Where are we going?" I asked.

"I want to show you something," he said.

"What?"

He turned and gave me an appraising look. "Let's just drive for a while, and then I'll tell you."

I sat quietly, my hands clenched together in my lap, staring straight ahead, my thoughts in disoriented slivers.

"Whatcha takin' in school this year?" he asked in a conversational tone that caught me off guard.

"Just the usual."

"Seniors still have as much fun as I did when I was a senior in high school?"

"I suppose."

"You in any of those little girl groups?"

I turned to face him. "They don't have 'little

girl groups' anymore. They have people groups
...people."

"And what do those people groups do?"

"You know. Spanish Club, Honor Society, Tennis Team—all those things."

"And the girls don't get together and giggle and
talk about boys anymore?"

"Well, yes. I mean no. That is, not exactly." I
was losing my patience. "Of course we talk about
boys, but we don't have clubs to do it in."

"Y'all still talk about who likes who—that sort
of stuff—the way the girls in my time used to do?"

"Sure ... I mean—"

His tone changed abruptly. "When y'all talked
about Sara, who did you say she liked?"

I looked at him, my lips parted, groping for the
right thing to say, but he quickly added, "Lauren,
don't you see how important it is for me to have
all the information?"

"Honestly," I said, "I don't know who Sara
liked. I just know that she was out a lot and—"

"And what?"

"She liked all sorts of guys ... men."

"Name me some names."

"Please," I said, twisting on the seat, "I can't
just give you names of people. It makes them
sound guilty just because she was talking to
them."

I thought about how Fant came through the
dark backyard to remind me that Sara went to
talk to Feenie. To Feenie. Was Fant afraid I'd

mention his name and get him in trouble with his wife? And I thought about Sara climbing out of Jep's pickup truck. Maybe he had just given her a ride home from school. I couldn't make a nice guy like Jep look guilty.

"Any man who was handy," I said. "Sara liked to talk to them all."

"And they all liked her the same?"

"Of course not."

"So who liked Sara the most?"

"Why do you ask me that?" I groaned. "It's so unfair!"

"Why is it unfair?"

"Because I only know of one guy at school who liked Sara a lot, and if I gave you his name, you'd be suspicious of him. And meanwhile, there might be other guys I don't even know about who were after Sara, and you wouldn't be suspicious of them."

"I have to track down all the leads I can. I talk to you, and I talk to others around town, and pretty soon, if I'm lucky, all the pieces fit together, and then I know where I'm goin'."

"I'm not going to tell you," I said. I turned to face forward and for the first time really noticed where we were.

The woods were thick at each side of the highway, the underbrush a matted tangle of vines and scrub, the pines so thick the bigger ones were choking out the spindly ones that struggled to grow upward.

"Why are we out here?" I leaned forward and clutched the dashboard.

"You been pretty closemouthed with your information," he said. "How come you want me to be free with mine?"

"I just want to know where you're taking me!"

"Just a ways up here," Sheriff Norvell said, and he slowed to turn left on a narrow dirt road that curved into the Thicket to make a turnaround for parking. He pulled the car to a stop and said, "Let's get out."

I did as he said, but my legs felt numb. I wondered if they'd hold me up.

"There's a path down this-away," he said. He waited for me.

"I'd rather stay here." I gripped the door handle.

"Lauren," he said, "come with me."

I couldn't move. What I wanted to do was turn and run down the highway, but I was so frightened that I seemed to be frozen in the spot. I could hear my own heart pounding loudly and it seemed out of rhythm with the sounds of the forest around us.

In a couple of strides Sheriff Norvell came to my side, took my right hand firmly in his left hand, and pulled me toward the Thicket. I was moving into a deep green spell with walls that would wrap around me like a shroud, the way they held Sara and Roberta, forever.

"The hunters come and park here, then take

this path," the sheriff said. His voice splintered the spell, and for the first time I realized that I didn't have to walk to whatever waited for me without a fight.

I jerked back my hand, and in surprise he let go. But he was blocking the way out of the Thicket, so I turned to run down the path ahead of him. I knew people had been lost forever by leaving the paths in the Thicket, but if I stayed carefully on the path, somewhere, somehow, it was bound to lead me out.

His voice boomed out, surrounding me. "Stop!" he shouted. "For God's sake, Lauren, don't move!"

The urgency halted me, and I turned to look at him. He had his gun in his hand.

"Don't move," he said quietly.

I closed my eyes. So this was the way it would be. I tried to think of a prayer, but my mind was blank, like an empty blotter soaking up the sounds and smells of the lush forest around me.

The gunshot hurt my ears. I squeezed my eyes tightly together, waiting, but there was no pain, no sensation of having been shot.

"You stupid girl!" Sheriff Norvell said next to my ear. "Look what you almost went and ran into!"

I opened my eyes and followed a direct line from his pointing finger to the floor of the trail a few feet ahead of me. A large black and gray cane-brake rattler lay splattered across the trail, its head blasted to an oozing pulp.

I held my hands to my face and stared at the sheriff. He stared back for a few minutes, his eyebrows in a furry frown. Finally, he said, "You were afraid of *me*, Lauren?"

"I thought you were going to kill me," I whispered.

"Why?"

"Because I knew that Sara was going out to meet someone, that she was going to leave town with him."

"She told you that?"

"Yes, but she never did tell me who he was. It could even have been you. I saw you pick her up one day after school."

For an instant he looked bewildered. Then he said, "I needed some information about her birthdate for the records. I pulled over to ask her, and she said she'd appreciate it if I'd give her a lift to the drugstore. Took maybe five, ten minutes."

"That was all? But where did she go all that afternoon? Who was she with?" I was talking not to the sheriff, but to myself.

His thoughts had moved on. He rubbed his chin and said, "Sara went far enough to tell you she was going away with someone. How come she didn't tell you his name? Wouldn't she have liked to brag a little?"

"I wondered about that," I said. "And then it came to me that if she didn't tell me, it was probably because she couldn't."

"Couldn't?"

"I mean, what if he was married, or someone important in town?"

He frowned at me, nodding, thoughts moving behind his eyes.

"Why did you bring me here?" I asked.

"I thought if you saw the spot where Sara was killed, you might feel like telling me who she met."

"I'd tell you if I knew!"

"Yes," he said. "I think now you would."

"I feel guilty enough about what happened to Sara. I'm the one who locked the door behind her and kicked the lamp plug out of the socket so it would take a few minutes for someone to turn on the light."

"I figured as much."

"Sara worked it out. She said it would give her time to get away. She said most of the superstitious people in town would think it was all something supernatural and get so carried away about spirits and stuff that they wouldn't come looking for her until the next morning." I lowered my head, embarrassed.

"The next morning," he said, "when one of the men in town also showed up missing?" He sighed. "Seems to me she made it harder for herself. Why couldn't she have just gone away on one of those evenings when she sneaked out of the house? No one would have missed her until the next morning."

"I've wondered about that," I answered. "I

guess Sara needed something special, some sort of notice taken of her. If she just quietly went away, who would know or care that much? This way it was . . . well, it was like a wedding, with the whole town in on it. It was the closest thing to a going-away party that Sara could hope for."

"Would you say that Roberta was the maid of honor?"

"Stop it!" I began to cry, clutching at my cheeks with clammy fingers. "Don't you think I feel guilty about Roberta, too? It should have been me! Not Roberta! The person who killed Sara thought Roberta had planned everything with her and knew who Sara was going to meet! Is that my fault? Tell me! I don't know! Is it? Is it?"

"Let's go back to town," Sheriff Norvell said.

I stopped crying. Hiccuping and sniffling, I tried to rub my nose with a fuzzy tissue I found in my jeans pocket. As I climbed into the car, I looked around. The afternoon sun would still be bright out on the road, but inside the Thicket the gloom seemed to smother us, foglike. By night the dark stench of damp, rotting leaves would be horrifying.

"Roberta?" I asked. "Where . . . ?" I couldn't finish the sentence.

"Another road," he said. "A little farther into the Thicket."

I shuddered.

"It could be you next, Lauren." His voice was a

husky drawl. "Some people think you know who Sara was goin' to meet."

"You're not telling me anything I don't know."

"Give it more thought. Go over the people you've seen Sara with. Give me some names."

I hesitated. "Jep let her out of his truck near the house once."

He stared at me, and his voice was like a bark, a scornful laugh. "Jep? My deputy? Maybe he gave her a ride back from school, somethin' like that. I asked for names, Lauren, not wild guesses."

I gripped my hands together. "That's what I mean! Any name I could give you would have as much meaning as Jep's! I can't give you names! I don't know any way to help!"

"Think about it," he said gruffly. He started the car, and we rode back to town. Just once he broke the silence between us by saying. "Y'know your life is in danger, Lauren."

I wanted to scream. I knew only too well that my life was in danger, but what was I going to do about it?

10

That night Aunt Mel came into the room where I was trying to work on my English lit homework. She had a half inch of pink stuff on her face, and as she talked, it squished around the corners of her mouth. Aunt Mel never wore a bit of makeup, but every night she religiously put cream on her face.

"This is a new kind that Emma Dawson sold me," she said. "It's full of vitamin E and keeps away wrinkles."

"You don't have any wrinkles, Aunt Mel," I said.

"Of course I don't, because I use the right kinds of creams," she said.

I had no answer for that.

The front doorbell rang, causing us both to start.

"You expecting anyone?" she asked.

"No," I said.

Aunt Mel frowned, and the cream rippled into little ridges. "If it's that fool Ashe Norvell again . . ." She strode to the front door and flung it open.

I was right behind her, and I was startled to see Jep Jackson. He took one look at Aunt Mel, and his mouth opened in a gaping, working motion like a new-caught catfish gulping air.

"I hoped to talk to y'all," he said, "but if you're real busy or going out or anything . . . ?" He let the question dangle.

I knew if I opened my mouth, I'd burst out laughing, so I kept quiet.

Aunt Mel forgot about the cream on her face. She held the door wide and stepped back. "It's a mite late," she said, "but come in, Jep, if you've got something on your mind."

We made a weird trio as Jep edged into the room and fumbled into a chair. He was obviously nervous. Aunt Mel, oblivious to the greasy pink mask she turned on him, peered through it with puzzled eyes. I couldn't look directly at Jep, so I studied a spot on the wall as though I were trying to memorize it for a test.

Here was a man I had dreamed about. A few weeks ago I would have given anything in the world to have Jep Jackson sitting in our living room, hoping he had come because of me.

Now I knew he had come because of me. There was no other reason. My face was hot and sticky, and I hated Sheriff Norvell for making me give him a name.

"There's something I think I need to explain to y'all," Jep said. He tried to look earnestly at Aunt Mel's pink face but seemed so disconcerted that he turned to me. "Sheriff Norvell told me that you said you'd seen Sara get out of my pickup truck."

The words were out, and I hiccuped in anguish. "I'm sorry, Jep! He insisted I give him names of men that Sara had been out with. I tried to tell him I couldn't! That I didn't want to put suspicion on anyone because I didn't know that much! But he kept after me, and I finally told him your name." I paused, rubbing my arms up and down the legs of my jeans until my palms stung. "Sheriff Norvell laughed at me."

"There was no call for him to do that," Aunt Mel said. "If you answered his question, he should have respected your answer."

"I didn't kill Sara, or Roberta either," Jep said. He had taken off his wide-brimmed felt hat and looked as though he were trying to cram it into a tight roll.

"I know you didn't, Jep!" I said. But at the same time I thought, "How can I say that? How could I know?"

133

Aunt Mel turned to Jep. "What's this about Sara and your truck? What does it mean?"

"Only what Lauren knows," Jep said. "Sara . . . well, Sara was a pretty girl, and lots of fun if you didn't take her seriously. And I . . . well, just a few times we drove over to that roadhouse the other side of the county line for a few beers for me and pop for her. Just soda pop, mind you. And I wanted to pick her up here and bring her back to y'all's because I wasn't ashamed of what I was doing. But she said you weren't really her guardian, and it made you no nevermind, so I—"

"You knew better than that, Jep," Aunt Mel said.

"I guess," he said. "Sorry."

"She was that kind of girl," Aunt Mel said.

He perked up and blinked at her.

"No need to beat around the bush. That's why she didn't stay long in any foster home. That's why her mother turned her over to the court. Nobody's fooling anyone by talking around what we all know."

Jep blushed, his normally sunburned face turning a deeper crimson. "Uh . . . yeah," he said.

"She was also a minor."

Jep looked as though he had been squashed flat.

"But enough of that," Aunt Mel said. "I'm going to get you a cup of coffee and some oatmeal cookies. What's over is over, and there's no point in ever bringing it up again."

Before he could answer, she was out of the room, and we could hear a bustle in the kitchen.

I was so dumbfounded by the conversation that I could only continue to stare at Jep, which didn't make either of us feel any better.

Jep tried to ease the situation. "So what's new?" he asked.

Hysteria is the name for it, I guess. I laughed until Aunt Mel came in and shook me and put cold cloths on my face and sent me up to bed. I didn't even say good-bye to Jep. I didn't want to. I lay in bed wondering what I had ever seen in him.

I curled up around the pillow, listening to Aunt Mel lock the doors, turn out the lights, and come up to bed. I could hear the comfortable, creaking noises of her bedsprings settling and finally the special quiet of a house that has burrowed down to sleep.

My eyelids were growing heavy, and I nuzzled my face into the pillow. Jep's confession. Blah. Who wanted to hear it? "Only what Lauren knows!" Ha!

But I didn't know! I didn't know any of what Jep told us. He thought I did. Or did he tell only what he thought I knew, leaving some of it out—something important—something about getting rid of a girl who demanded too much from him?

And maybe his visit wasn't just to make amends to Aunt Mel. Maybe it was to serve as a warning to me!

"Not you, Jep!" I thought. But Jep wasn't the person I had imagined him to be in all my day-dreams about him. I didn't know who Jep was. He could be anyone. He could even be the murderer!

11

School the next day was a disaster. I kept falling asleep in class. I'd have dreams about Sara and Roberta. I wished Roberta's family had buried her here instead of taking her body back to Louisiana. It was like an unfinished painting or a song in which you can't remember the last line.

Maddie, Luemma, and Dana avoided one another and me. Allie, as a best friend would, clung to me. I sat with her at lunchtime in the cafeteria, where the greasy smell of deep-fried okra hung over the peanut-butter sandwich I had brought from home, making me want to gag. Allie had bought the special of the day, which included a limp lettuce salad, a bowl of the okra that looked as though it were bleeding green through its shell of pale batter, and a meat concoction that was any-one's guess.

"How can you eat that?" I asked her.

"With a spoon," she said. "You really need a spoon, because the sauce is so runny, and—"

"Never mind," I said. "It doesn't look good."

"It doesn't taste so bad once you get used to it," she said, and I remembered that Allie's mother wasn't a very good cook.

"Let's get together after school," I said. "I need to talk to you."

She stopped eating, brushed back the frizzed ends of her hair that had just missed dipping into the okra, and looked at me suspiciously. "Lauren," she said, "I don't want to talk about—well, you know."

"I need someone who was there," I said. "I need you to help me put together the pieces."

"No," she said flatly. "I can't bear thinking about it, so I'm not going to talk about it."

"But if it would help me?"

She reached across the table and patted my hand and sandwich, getting her fingers full of peanut butter. "Lauren, I would do anything in the world to help you. But not that. Why don't we talk about other things? Fun things?"

I could only nod agreement at the brightness in her eyes, and she went back to eating the daily poison potion, oblivious of the way I felt.

Allie took her tray back to the kitchen, and I finished my sandwich, wondering why I felt uncomfortable. Finally, I realized that someone was watching me. I looked up and around the cafeteria quickly. Carley Hughes was sitting a couple of tables away. His steady eyes met mine.

When I glanced at him he smiled tentatively, wadded up his lunch bag, and threw it into the nearby trash can. Some cutesy freshman applauded and grinned and did everything but flutter her eyelashes. He ignored her and came to sit next to me.

"Thanks for visiting my grandmother the other day," he said. "It meant a lot to her. She gets lonely."

It took a few moments for me to remember my visit to Ila Hughes. "Oh," I said. "Yes. She asked me to come by and talk to her, so I did."

"You didn't stay long. She said for me to tell you to come back."

"Well," I stammered, not looking at him, "she just wanted to know about the séance that night, and there wasn't much I could tell her and—"

"Oh, no," he interrupted. "Don't get her wrong. She isn't just a curious old lady. She probably didn't know what you'd want to talk about."

He rubbed one finger on the edge of the table, picking at a stubby splinter with his nails. "She works awful hard in the café, and I work, too, and we don't get much time together. The customers josh her, but mostly they don't really talk to her. She's too busy to go to women's clubs and stuff like that. And she's had differences with some of

139

the neighbors. She really likes it when someone comes by."

"I guess I misunderstood."

"Yeah," Carley said. He smiled at me again. "You come by and see her whenever you've got some free time and she's home on a break. She likes you, Lauren. She says you're a nice girl, the kind who'll make something of herself."

My returning smile faded. "Make what of myself? I've got to face facts, Carley. Next June we'll be graduating, and then I'll have to get a full-time job. The dime store, where I work summers and Christmas vacation, offered me a place, but I don't know. I hate to think of spending my whole life working there."

"How about college?"

"I'm not an A-student. I can't hope for a full scholarship. The money from my vacation jobs has gone to help at home; so I haven't saved enough to do any good. Just the board bill at any state college would be fierce. I can't ask Aunt Mel to do that for me. If we had a college in town it might be different, but we don't."

"You make it sound so hopeless," he said. "There are lots of people who take it a little slower and work their way through."

"Work and live in a strange city?" The idea scared me.

I felt as though I were having the same conversation I'd had with Jep in the supermarket. No matter how much it hurt, I had made up my mind not to hope for college. And now people were asking me to consider it. I was confused, and it disturbed me.

"Don't you want to go to college?"

"Of course I do—very much. But I decided to be practical and accept a few facts. Just because you're going on a scholarship—"

Allie came back to the table. "Hi, Carley," she said.

He stood up and nodded. "Hi, Allie. See y'all later."

Allie watched him stride toward the door. "I didn't mean to break anything up," she apologized.

"You didn't." I picked up my books, crumpled the trash from my lunch, and dropped it into the splattered can as we left the room. "He just wanted to ask me to visit his grandmother again."

"His grandmother?" Allie made a face. "What kind of guy asks a girl to visit his grandmother instead of inviting her to a movie or something?"

"His grandmother is lonely," I said. "I went to see her once before, and she wants me to come back."

"You don't want to visit old Mrs. Hughes. She's strange."

Maybe it was the way I felt about Allie's not coming through when I needed her. Maybe it was just because I was in a bad mood and felt like doing the opposite of what anyone suggested. "Yes, I

141

do," I said. "I'm going after school today—before she has to go on dinner shift at the café."

"I thought you were coming over to my house," Allie said.

"Tomorrow."

"Tomorrow I have band practice, and if I miss one more time, Mr. Peters is going to take away my triangle."

"Allie," I said, "here's my history class. I'll call you later." I didn't want to visit Carley's grandmother, but now I had talked myself into a corner. I had no choice. I just hoped Carley wouldn't be there.

But he was.

I dawdled on the way. I was mad at the whole world, including myself, and took it out by stamping on crunchy leaves and kicking the battered pieces into the street. It didn't help my mood when I knocked on the back screen door and Carley answered instead of his grandmother.

He looked at me with surprise, and I said, "I came to see your grandmother. You asked me to."

"I didn't think you'd come so soon."

"I didn't either. But I thought . . . well, is she here?"

Carley suddenly remembered that he hadn't even opened the screen door, pushed it open too fast, and banged it into my arm. "I'm sorry," he said. "Come on in. She'll be back in a minute." He had my elbow in one hand and was squeezing me into the house in spite of my mumbled protests that I'd come back later.

"Look, if she's not home, then I might as well come another day." I was wedged against the doorframe, tugging back, but it was an unequal contest.

"What's the matter with you, Lauren?" Carley asked. "You're not afraid to be alone with me for a few minutes, are you?"

I suppose that's exactly what I was afraid of. I couldn't tell him that it was like being out in a field with a norther coming toward me and the sky turning that deep, cold blue, spreading wider and higher as it came closer and closer. Only now it was danger that was sweeping toward me. I couldn't see the face behind the danger any more than I could see a face in the penetrating cold of the norther. The danger, if it reached me, would freeze me out, and I was terrified.

Carley had gone out with Sara, too. Why should I trust Carley?

"Sit down," Carley said. "I'll get you something to drink. Want a Coke?"

He had his head in the refrigerator by this time, so I inched my way toward the table, put down my books, and slowly eased into one of the wooden kitchen chairs.

Carley was just turning around when the screen door opened and closed with a bang and Ila Hughes came into the room.

"Lauren! What a nice surprise!" she said. She

was peering over a brown paper sack with green fronds waving out the top, and she handed it to Carley. "Miz Jeffers gave me some collard from her garden. Just stick these in the refrigerator, will you, Carley?"

She sat across from me and smoothed out her cotton skirt. "You left so soon after you come before, Lauren, that we didn't get down to a real chat. Before too long Carley will be graduating and going off to college, and I'll be glad for some young people coming around to say hello. I hope you'll stop by often."

Carley handed me a glass, said something about having to get to practice, and left. I began to relax.

The kitchen was too warm, and the faded curtains at the window were a long way from the bright-yellow polka dots they once were. A bunch of once-green leaves were laid out in the sun on the windowsill to dry, and they were twisted and curled as the moisture inside them was squeezed out. Over on the mantel of the fireplace the row of little bird skulls stared down like so many little ghosts.

Suddenly Mrs. Hughes reached across the table and clasped my right hand, pulling it toward her, spreading my fingers flat against the tabletop. "You've got good fingers," she said. "You've got a strong healing finger."

"A what?"

"Your ring finger." She tapped it. "This finger
144

has healing powers. Never apply medicaments with your forefinger. It's a poison finger." She leaned toward me. "Lots of folks don't know that."

"I didn't know," I managed to say. Her hands were dry, like fine sandpaper against my hand.

She studied my hands for a few more moments without saying a word. I didn't speak either, and I didn't draw my hand away. I don't know why.

Just as suddenly as she had taken my hand, she released it, and I drew it protectively into my lap.

"How's Melvamay?" Mrs. Hughes asked.

"Fine," I said.

"This all has been a strain on her," she said. "It's hard enough raising your own without raising other people's children."

I guess I blushed because she quickly added, "Oh, I didn't mean you, Lauren. You're just like you was Melvamay's own."

I didn't like the direction the conversation was taking. "Mrs. Hughes, I really don't want to talk right now about Sara and Roberta."

"I should imagine not, poor child," she said. "With the sheriff pestering you to give him information, and people wanting to know all the details, and you keeping so much inside for fear of hurting people."

"What do you mean? Keeping what inside?"

"Oh, my," she said. "I didn't mean to get you upset."

"Please, Mrs. Hughes," I said, trying to relax, "let's talk about something else. Everyone thinks I know something about who killed Sara, and I don't. The murderer thought Roberta knew something, and she didn't."

Mrs. Hughes looked surprised. "Oh, I've got you riled, and I didn't mean to do it."

But it was as though a floodgate had been opened. I leaned across the table toward her, gripping the edge as hard as I could. It was pressing painfully into my rib cage, and I didn't care. The words poured out. "Roberta was an innocent victim. She was playing séance just to get people to pay attention to her. She didn't know what Sara was going to do. Sara told me she was sure Roberta would turn out the lights and have candles or something because she'd seen a séance on television or in the movies or somewhere. I was going to make sure the plugs to any lamps were pulled out of the wall, and when Sara put out the candles, I'd let her out the front door and lock it behind her. Sara went out to meet someone and run away with him. And Roberta didn't know who it was! Roberta didn't know a thing about it, and she got killed! And it was my fault!" My voice was almost a shriek when I finished.

We stared at each other across the table like two hypnotized chickens at a carny show. In the silence of the kitchen I could hear a car hum by on the roadway, the buzz of a bee batting against the window screen, and the sudden creak of a floorboard by the kitchen door.

I half rose from my chair, whirling in self-defense. It was Carley. He let out a long breath and said, "I didn't mean to eavesdrop. I came back to get my cleats. You were talking and . . ."

"I was talking too much," I said. I turned to Mrs. Hughes. "I'm sorry I let off steam. I shouldn't have done it. Maybe when this is all over, I'll be better company."

I tucked my books into my left arm and moved toward the door.

"Wait," she said. "You haven't finished your drink, Lauren. Don't run off."

"Next time," I said. "When this is over."

She got up and moved toward me slowly. "It will never be over," she answered. The tone of her voice frightened me.

"When evil is let loose, how do you stop it?" She looked as though she were going to cry. "Because a group of foolish girls pried into the dark things of the other world, two of them are dead."

"No!" I said. "It wasn't like that!"

"The evil is like a flood that begins with a few drops, then gets stronger and stronger until it covers people and smothers people and sweeps them up and carries them away, and there is no stopping the flood."

"It wasn't evil!" I gasped. "We were just playing a game."

"You don't play with supernatural forces," she said.

Carley took a step forward. "Grandma, you're scaring the daylights out of Lauren. Cut it out."

147

I shook my head as though trying to shake away a nightmare. Without even saying good-bye I dashed out of the house and ran down the road until I reached home. I was more frightened than I had ever been in my life.

12

I had just finished the dinner dishes and hung up the dishtowel, puttering a bit at putting the canisters straight along the back of the kitchen counter, when the doorbell rang.

"I'll get it," Aunt Mel said quickly, but I followed her into the hall. I was as curious as she was to find who was at the door this time of evening.

The porch light, with its antimosquito globe, washed Carley Hughes's face with a violent, sickly yellow.

"Come on in, Carley," Aunt Mel said, stepping aside. "I take it you came to see Lauren and not me."

She turned to get me, but I was right at her elbow. My heart was thumping. What was Carley doing here?

"Hi," he said, trying to look cheerful with a smile that flapped on and off like a flag in the wind. "I'd like to talk to you, Lauren."

He looked nervously toward Aunt Mel, but she got the message and said, "Y'all sit down here in the living room. I've got some things to get done in the kitchen."

Carley slowly lowered himself into a chair, and I eased sideways into the sofa, perched stiffly as far from Carley as I could manage.

"First of all, I'm sorry Grandma scared you this afternoon," he said. "It was real nice of you to go visit her, Lauren. I didn't know she'd act like that."

"She thinks it was devils who killed Sara," I mumbled.

"Not really," he said. "She talks about evil forces and stuff, especially when she's with that Mrs. Granbery, but down inside she must know that Sara and Roberta weren't just spirited away."

"They were murdered," I said. "And I really don't want to talk to you about it."

"I know how you feel," he said. "But I overheard what you told my grandmother, and it made me decide that I had to come and tell you something."

"Tell me something? What everyone else has been telling me? That you suspect I know who killed Sara Martin?"

He looked at me with such anguish that I wanted to cry out.

"No," he said. "You don't know who killed Sara, but I do."

I leaned forward, holding my breath. "Who was it?"

"I killed her," Carley said. His eyes got red, and he rubbed his nose vigorously before he could say anything else. I couldn't even move, let alone answer him.

"I'm the one Sara was supposed to meet that night," Carley finally said. His voice wavered and cracked, but he got control and added, "I don't know what there was about her. We were—well, I thought it made sense our being together. She said we could go to the city and both of us work and be together all the time." He put his head in his hands and cried for a few minutes, rubbing his nose now and then on his shirtsleeves.

I managed to get to my feet, go into the bathroom, and bring back a box of tissues, shoving it into his hands. I wanted to comfort him, but I couldn't. I wanted to say just the right words to him, but nothing formed in my mind. The thoughts in my head weren't making sense.

"Why did you drown her?" I finally whispered. I wasn't sure I was the one asking the question, but it seemed to come from me.

Carley sat up, gave a final wipe to his nose, and stared at me. "I didn't drown her!"

"But the autopsy report said—"

He shook his head violently. "No, Lauren. What I'm trying to tell you is that I had it all set up to meet Sara. I knew she was going to Roberta's house for something. She didn't say it was a séance. I didn't know she was going to go through that disappearing act. I had a bag packed in the back of that car I use to get to work, and I was going to pick her up out on the highway."

"Why on the highway?"

"That was her idea. I don't know why. Sara worked out the plan. God! It doesn't make any sense now that I'm telling somebody about it!"

"You got there and Sara wasn't there?"

"I didn't get there until late. Mr. Glade, who owns the café, had to go into Beaumont on business, and he asked Grandma to close up for him, so she was late getting the car home."

It dawned on me. "You were going to run away in your grandmother's car?"

He looked defensive. "It's my car. She gave it to me when I was old enough to get my license. We shared it . . . that is . . . Oh, Lauren, I feel rotten enough about what happened. Don't you think this has been driving me crazy?"

"What did you do when you found out Sara wasn't there?"

"I drove around, looking for her. I went by Roberta's, but the house was dark. Finally, I just went home. Sara was kind of . . . well, I thought she had changed her mind. I was afraid to phone her to ask to talk to her because it was so late. Then in the morning I heard she had disappeared."

"Have you told your grandmother about this? Or the sheriff?"

He groaned. "I haven't had enough courage to tell anyone. My grandmother would hate me. The sheriff would slap me in jail and be sure I was the one who had done the real killing."

I watched Carley for a few minutes. "But you told me."

"Yeah," he said. "I felt I owed you that much." He leaned back in his chair, and I could see that some of the tension had disappeared from his face.

"You aren't in a very good spot either," he said. "Everyone thinks you know a lot more than you're telling. I was pretty sure you knew about Sara and me—about our seeing each other at night sometimes and all that."

"I didn't know," I said. "I didn't like Sara. We didn't confide in each other."

Aunt Mel was perking coffee, and the fragrance was seeping into the living room, tantalizing me. I nodded in the direction of the kitchen. "Want a cup?"

"Sure," he said. "Black."

It took a few minutes to get the coffee and bring it to the living room. Carley was sitting in the same position, staring into space.

"Did you love Sara, Carley?" I asked, sitting close to him and putting the coffee cups on a low table. This time I reached out and touched his hand.

He took my hand and gripped it. "Yeah," he said. "I guess I did."

"What are you going to do now?"

He gave a long, painful sigh. "I suppose I'll talk to the sheriff. I feel a lot cleaner inside now. Talking to you has helped a lot. You're a good friend."

For the first time we smiled at each other. I reached over and handed him his cup of coffee, although I really wanted to keep my hand in his. He was comforting me. I was comforting him. I liked that.

Carley and I were sitting there, sipping coffee, easy with each other, when a loud knock on the front door made us jump. We both went to answer it, as though we were a mutual protection society.

Fant Lester burst past me into the house as soon as I opened the door. "Where's Mel?" he asked me, ignoring Carley.

"Coming, coming," she called, bustling into the hall behind me. "What's the problem, Fant?"

"It's Feenie," he said. "I think she's having a gallbladder attack."

"Did you call the doctor?"

"Yep, but he's not back from a meeting he went to in Houston. They said it would be another hour."

"Shouldn't you take her to the hospital?"

"It's too long a drive. Feenie said the pain isn't that bad, and she wants to wait for the doctor." He looked as helpless as the rabbits he liked to

154

pick off at night with a shotgun and a spotlight, freezing them into tiny statues with wide glassy eyes.

"You want me to come over and see what I can do?" Aunt Mel asked him.

"Oh, would you, Mel? I'm no good at this!" He sighed and seemed to collapse.

"It's all right, Fant," Aunt Mel said, reaching out to steady him. "You go home to Feenie, and I'll be over in a few minutes."

She shut the door behind him and eyed Carley and me. "It's not proper to leave you two alone in the house together, with no chaperone. Whyn't you move on out to the front porch and finish your conversation there?"

I felt myself blushing. "Aunt Mel, we were just talking."

"And so would the town if they knew you were alone in the house together," she said bluntly.

I wanted to turn invisible on the spot, but Carley just nodded and said, "You're right." He opened the door and went out on the porch.

I followed him, glad that there was a thick layer of clouds snuffing out the moonlight, that it was so dark Carley couldn't see the expression on my face. Aunt Mel was right behind us.

"Shouldn't be more'n an hour or so," she said. "I'll come home after the doctor gets there."

Aunt Mel reached for the switch to the porch light, but I put my hand over it and looked at her beseechingly. I was not going to sit with Carley under a glaring bug light.

She shut the door behind us and disappeared into the blackness. We could hear the gate squeak and her shoes clopping down the sidewalk. There was just a faint shadow where she moved under the trees. I sat on the top step, pulling my knees up under my chin. Carley sat next to me, close enough so that our hips were touching.

"I suppose we ought to talk about what we should do," I murmured. That really wasn't what I wanted to talk to Carley about. I hoped he wouldn't say anything more about Sara.

I wondered why I should let myself feel so responsive to Carley when he had come only to tell me he had almost run off with another girl; but every inch of my body was tuned in to him, enjoying his nearness, yearning for him. It was a purely physical sensation, but for some reason Carley's presence was more consoling to me than anyone else's could have been.

"In the morning I guess I'll go talk to the sheriff," Carley said.

"You'd better not," I said quickly. "I've been thinking about it, and I'm sure it could be the worst thing to do."

He turned toward me in the darkness, and his breath was warm on my cheek. "Why? I've got to tell him sometime."

"But not now," I said. "You know what he'd think. You said so yourself. You were out there on

156

the highway, driving around, no alibi, no one to prove you didn't kill Sara. He'd think it was you and stop looking for the real killer."

"Maybe he'll never find the real killer. It might be some guy who picked up Sara as a hitchhiker, and now he's hundreds of miles away from here."

"No," I said. "Don't forget Roberta. The same person who killed Sara killed Roberta because he thought she knew too much about him. It had to be someone from around here."

"Who?" he asked.

"You don't think I've wondered? I've tried to think over and over about the men I'd seen with Sara. I know there were others, probably lots of others, and—" I stopped, embarrassed. "I shouldn't have said that. I'm sorry."

"Don't be," Carley said. "I knew it. I knew it even when . . . I just didn't want to think about it."

"Carley," I said, leaning against him and liking the warmth of his body against mine, "let's talk about something else. Let's pretend that you came over just to see me, and for no other reason. Let's talk about school and what you're going to do in college and all that. Okay?"

"Why not?" Carley said.

"Have you decided which university you'll go to?"

"My first choice is A & M," he said. "They've offered me a full scholarship. How about you?"

There was that uncomfortable question again. I

fielded it. "Tell me about A & M," I said. "What's it like?"

We sat there for nearly half an hour, talking about college and classes and trivia and relaxing against each other and pretending everything was all right with a couple of lives, which, at the moment, were really messed up.

Finally, Carley stood up and said, "Time to go. Grandma will be getting back from the café. She likes me to be home when she gets there."

"It's going to work out all right," I said.

I could barely see him frowning at me in the darkness. "Games aren't any good, Lauren. They all have to end. Right now we've got a problem."

"What problem?"

"Your aunt isn't back, and I don't want to leave you alone."

"It's okay. I'm not worried."

"You want me to take you next door to the Lester house?"

"No, Carley. Honest. I'll go inside, and I'll be fine. Why should I be afraid?" I had a few good reasons why, and now that Carley had brought up my being alone, I didn't like the idea one bit. But Carley had problems of his own, and I wasn't going to add to them.

Carley walked to the front door and opened it. "I'll just check around," he said.

He went inside before I could stop him. I hurried and caught up with him in the kitchen. "There's no one in here," I said. "We were sitting on the front porch. We would have seen anyone who tried to break in."

He shrugged and grinned at me. "I guess it was just a gesture, just something to make me feel I wasn't walking off and leaving you without any protection."

I tugged at his hand. "Come on. I'll lock the front door behind you."

He paused on the threshold and took my hands. "Thanks for listening, Lauren. Thanks for being a good friend."

"Good night, Carley," I said. There was so much more I wanted to say, so much more I wanted than being just Carley's friend. But now was not the time to let him know it. Quickly I shut the door and bolted it.

I walked back into the kitchen and gulped down a glass of water. I leaned on the edge of the sink and tried to get everything back into perspective.

Then I heard it. From the living room came the soft pat of a footstep, a quiet, chilling, stealthy sound. I didn't breathe. I didn't move. Someone was in the house, and that someone was as still as I was, waiting, listening, aware that the old, hardwood floor had recorded his step.

I looked toward the phone. Not enough time. I would have to get out of the house, and quickly. As I ran toward the back door and threw it open, I realized that the living-room light had been turned off and the back door was unlocked.

Whoever was in the house had come in by way of the back door. Aunt Mel had left in such a hurry she probably hadn't thought to lock it.

But Carley had checked. Hadn't he? Or had I stopped him before he came to the back door and tried the knob?

As I stumbled down the back steps, the kitchen light flipped off. For a moment I stood motionless, wondering where I should go.

Nothing is as dark as a country town when the moon is hidden and most early risers have turned off their lights and gone to bed; so I launched myself into all that blackness with caution, walking gingerly, reaching out ahead to protect myself.

It wasn't until I was under the oak tree that I began to tremble. I realized that someone had come in that back door, opening it with silent hands, listening to what Carley and I were saying to each other, waiting for Carley to leave, knowing I'd be alone in the house.

First it was Sara who was murdered, then Roberta. Now was it going to be me?

13

It was terrifying not to know who was in that house, waiting for me. It was like a nightmare in which a creature without eyes and nose and mouth is coming toward you, and you want to run, but your feet don't move; and you want to scream, but your mouth won't make a sound.

My mind reached out to the someone in the house, to the faceless spider in the web. "If I knew who you were, I could fight down the panic. I'd try to plan how to fight you. It's not being able to put a face on you that's so terribly frightening."

I began to realize that I was breathing in little gasps, and I deliberately tried to make myself relax so that I could think clearly. I edged back, leaning against the tree, my eyes wide against the darkness. My mind plucked thoughts from the air as they passed, examining them, cataloguing them, or tossing them back into oblivion.

"He's inside the house. The back door was probably open. We've never had to be careful about locked doors before. Aunt Mel locks them before she goes to bed. It wasn't locked. Someone could have come in."

Who?

Fant could have left his house, left Feenie and Aunt Mel, and neither woman would have paid attention to his whereabouts. He could move through the soft grass behind our houses, slip through the hedge, creep up the back porch steps one at a time, put his hand carefully on the doorknob and turn it softly . . . gently . . . open it and slip inside.

It wouldn't have to be Fant. Jep had made his peace. Aunt Mel would remember that. No one would suspect Jep. He's a tall man, and strong, Jep is. He could take a girl into the Thicket and hold her under the water until she couldn't breathe and . . . If he parked one street over he could cut through the yard behind us, know-ing—as everyone in town knows—that old Mr. Barto would be asleep, wouldn't hear soft, pad-ding footsteps going up his drive and through the springy grass and around the rose bushes and across our yard and slowly, one step at a time, up the stairs, until his hand was on the doorknob. But if it's not Jep?

Who?

Someone no one has thought of? Some hairy-armed, beer gulper from the roadhouse out past the county line? One of those men who gather in noisy groups, sour sweat stains under their armpits, guck under their fingernails, yelling at each other until they get into their pickup trucks, with their CB antennas and their crude bumper stickers. They drive through town, calling rude comments to the girls, and maybe one of them picked up Sara. Maybe more than once. Maybe he thought I knew who he was, that Roberta knew.

"Who are you?" I whispered.

Someone heard me! I could feel it. The person who had locked me out of the house wasn't inside waiting for me. He was there, somewhere in the yard.

The two of us, blind as the bats that go screaming out of their caves at sunset, were as aware of each other in that yard as though we had the special antennae that bats use to find each other.

Part of my mind kept reaching out: "Where are you? Give me a clue!"

And part of it calmly kept repeating: "Stay away from the back of the house. Go to the front gate. Don't try to get to Aunt Mel, just in case the person in the yard is Fant."

"Where should I go?" My thoughts were frantic.

"Run," I answered. "Run as hard and fast as you can to town, to the sheriff's office."

"He won't be there."

163

"Sometimes he sleeps at the office. Jep might be there."

"Jep might be near me in the darkness, waiting to kill me."

I began to edge toward the front gate, out from under the protection of the tree. I moved an inch at a time. My eyes ached with the strain of trying to pierce the darkness to see who was with me. He must be wearing dark clothes. So far he's invisible.

I looked down at myself. My jeans were dark, but over my navy blue T-shirt I was wearing a white blouse.

Big mistake!

I silently, quickly unbuttoned the blouse and slipped it off. A separate thought, darting into my mind, told me not to drop it on the ground, but to hang it on a nearby branch, at a spot near my height. I spread the arms out, working fast and glancing over my shoulder. If the person hiding in the darkness were keeping track of me with my white blouse, then maybe this would give me a head start. Maybe he'd see it and think I was still under the tree. It was a chance.

I moved away from the tree. I stepped slowly and carefully toward the front of the house. I'd take a few steps and stop and listen. Sometimes I heard a small noise. Sometimes I only thought I heard a noise. Little night sounds, scurryings in the grass, crickets chirping under the back hedge, creeping things, crawling things. Tonight I could hear them.

But I couldn't hear the person who was with me.

I wanted to scream so badly the thought was almost overpowering me. Somehow the energy of that scream moved to my legs, and I ran frantically the last few feet, flinging myself through the grass toward the front gate.

The gate stuck, and I tugged at it. But a hand gripped my left arm and spun me backward. An arm was around my neck, my chin caught tightly in the crook of an elbow. My left arm was jerked upward, twisted painfully against my backbone.

As my head was pulled back I could barely see, parked in the street directly in front of me, Carley's old dented car, the car I could recognize without a doubt.

"Oh, no, Carley! Not you! I believed you! It couldn't be you!"

I was being pushed toward the car, but I wasn't going to give up without a fight. When they found my body, they were going to know that I had struggled with all my might. I wasn't going to make this easy.

I couldn't move my head, and my left arm was twisted backward at such a painful angle I couldn't bend it, so I used my feet. I kicked backward with all my strength until I connected with bone.

The cry in my ear was shrill. "Stop that! I've got a gun! I'll shoot you here and now! Stop!"

It wasn't the threat. It was the voice that spoke it. I froze.

"You're Mrs. Hughes! You're Carley's grandmother!"

"And you're a tool of evil," she hissed at me. "You and those other girls—trying to sway Carley into the wrong path, trying to take him from what he should be doing. I've got a gun in my hand, Lauren. I mean what I said about shooting you if you give me trouble."

It was hard to talk with my head twisted back. This crazy woman was incredibly strong. I managed to make my voice as calm as I could and say, "Mrs. Hughes, I don't want to hurt Carley. I don't want to bother him."

She snorted. "He was going to run off with that Sara, that tramp! I heard them talking! I saw the bag of Carley's things in the trunk of the car! Well, she didn't go nowhere with him. Did she?"

"But Carley—"

She didn't hear me. "Roberta, too! Those Cajuns have spells to put on people, you know. She was going to put a spell on Carley. You told me she didn't know all about him going to run away with Sara, but she was helping Sara with that séance and her spells. She was up to something."

"Why don't we sit down and talk about this?" I asked, then realized what an inane remark it was to make to a woman who was acting like a maniac.

"Get in the car," she said. "If you want to talk to me, you can do it while we're driving."

"You don't want to kill me, Mrs. Hughes," I said. She was propelling me toward the car, pushing me against the door, and while I talked to her, my mind was frantically trying to figure out what I could do to help myself.

"You drive the car," she said.

"I can't drive," I told her.

Her face was now up against mine, and her eyes glittered like dark water. "Oh, yes, you can. Don't lie to me. All you kids have to take driver's ed in school nowdays. I know you can drive."

I slid in behind the wheel. Maybe I had a chance after all. If we went through town . . .

She was like a witch who could see into my mind. "This time we're going out a side road to a place where they won't find your body for a long, long time. You'll lie in the swamp, decaying, thinking of your sins, and maybe they'll never find your body!"

"Why do you want to kill me?" The words were thick and slow. The steering wheel was damp under my hands, and the gun was hurting my side where she was pressing, jabbing it into me.

"You knew about Carley and Sara, too," she murmured. "Sara would have told you. No, no, no. Carley has to be able to go off to college and make something of himself, without anybody remembering that girl Sara and what she tried to

167

trick him into doing. Since you know, I'm going to make you forget."

"But Sara hadn't told me anything," I began.

"Start the car," she said. "Turn it around, and go out the road away from town."

If I struggled with her I'd be shot. If I drove out of town, I'd be killed, too. There was only one thing left to do. I started the car, floored the accelerator, twisted the wheel, and shot through the Lesters' picket fence, across their wide lawn, smack against the side of their brick house and into a hole of unconsciousness that mercifully swallowed me.

14

───────────

When I woke up in the hospital in Beaumont, all I knew was that I had been lulled with pain pills, I had a tongue too thick for my mouth, and Aunt Mel was sitting beside my bed.

Later I discovered that I had a mild concussion and a real pain in my right leg where a bullet had gone through.

"No lasting damage," Aunt Mel said, her knitting needles clacking at such a fast pace they seemed to be waving at each other.

"What happened to Mrs. Hughes?" I asked her.

"Not more than a few scratches on her." Aunt Mel's lips tightened, and I knew what she was thinking. "They've sent her downstate for psychiatric testing. Somebody'll decide she went way over the edge, and she'll probably never come to trial."

"It's just as well," I said. I stared up at the ceiling and thought about how awful this would be for Carley. A trial would make it even worse.

"What will Carley do?" I finally asked.

The needles paused. "He's of age. I imagine he'll stay on in town until after graduation from high school. Maybe after that he'll sell the house when he goes away to college."

"And never come back," I thought to myself. "Aunt Mel," I said, "you're not telling me how he's taking all this."

"It's hard on him, of course, but he'll come through." She added, "He's been real worried about you."

I didn't answer, and she said, "Although after he goes off to whatever university he chooses, you probably won't see each other again." She was looking at me carefully.

"Unless I go, too," I said. I surprised myself with the positive feelings I had, and I guess I surprised Aunt Mel, too.

"You, Lauren?" she asked. "You're thinking of going to college?"

I rolled over, stifling a groan, and propped myself on one elbow, so I could look directly into her eyes. "Aunt Mel, I know I haven't been working for grades, and I can't get a scholarship; but I do know I could try harder, and spend more time studying, and get a job to put myself through."

170

"You're a smart girl, Lauren," Aunt Mel said. "I've known all along that you didn't work on your grades as hard as you could, but I thought you just weren't that interested in school."

"I spent a lot of time thinking that high school was all there was going to be for me," I told her. "Now I know I can at least try for something else."

"You won't have to struggle alone," Aunt Mel said. Now the knitting fell to her lap, and she folded her hands together. "I've put away most of the money you earned with your summer and Christmas jobs, and there's no reason why I can't sell off that piece of grazing land that Amos Swantner's been wanting for so long."

She nodded, as though sealing an agreement with herself. "I've been realizing lately that you need to reach out beyond what you'd get here, Lauren. I've been selfish wanting you around, because . . ." Her voice dropped. "Because I love you."

I reached out and grabbed one of her hands, and her fingers returned the pressure. There was an energy flowing between us, an electricity of intense joy and excitement so strong I wondered if my body were glowing. It was a strange place to feel this way, but I was sure that this was the best moment in my life, having Aunt Mel there in the rickety old hospital chair, looking as though she wanted nothing else but to be with me.

171

After a while Aunt Mel said, "Carley wants to come and see you."

"I'd like that," I answered.

Carley could come, and I would be glad to see him, but right now I had all I needed or wanted. I was cared for. I was loved. I drifted off to sleep, holding tightly to Aunt Mel's hand.